Art Myatt

and The Little Green Dragon

Titles available in the Art Myatt series

(in reading order):

Art Myatt and The Jewel of the Sun

Art Myatt and The Little Green Dragon

Art Myatt

and The Little Green Dragon

PETER KAVANAGH

Copyright © 2013 by Peter Kavanagh

ISBN-13: 978-1494200503
ISBN-10: 1494200503

For Emma, Tom and Isla

Prologue

THE LITTLE GREEN DRAGON is the second children's adventure story in the Art Myatt series.

Art Myatt, Amy and a dog called Mr Beagle all meet again in the Oxfordshire village of Brillion after Amy invites Art to a Brillion fun weekend. There are many different events taking place at the fun weekend and people from all over Oxfordshire visit to take part.

The Little Green Dragon is lost and Art is asked to keep him safe and away from public interest for a few days. The problem is, because of the fun weekend, there is a lot more activity taking place in Brillion than normal. Art's task is hampered as The Little Green Dragon gets stronger and wants to be free to explore Brillion.

Some of the characters from the first book, THE JEWEL Of THE SUN, are re-introduced along with the introduction of new characters to make a brand new and exciting adventure.

CHAPTER ONE

AN INVITATION

The weather forecasters predicted sunshine for today. That's what Art's mother told him at breakfast. Art didn't really mind as long as he could go and stay with his Aunt Hayley in 'Honeypot Cottage' and see his friend Amy in the Oxfordshire village of Brillion. It was a short school holiday and Amy had invited him to a summer fun weekend at Brillion. He was really looking forward to a break from school homework and having some fun. It was Thursday morning and his mother was dropping him off before returning to pick him up on Monday the following week.

He sat on his bed with his suitcase packed reading a local Oxfordshire rugby magazine when his mother shouted to him from downstairs.

'Art, have you seen my car keys?'

'They're on the kitchen table Mum,' shouted Art, returning to read his magazine.

Art looked at the magazine turning the pages quickly looking for the picture of his team when he heard the telephone ring in the hallway downstairs. His mother answered the call and Art could tell by the tone of her voice something was wrong. The telephone call ended and Mrs Myatt slowly walked upstairs to Art's bedroom.

'Art, that was your Aunt Hayley. Mr Beagle's gone missing and she's very worried about him,' she said. 'We had better get going soon so we can help her find him. Have you packed everything you need?'

'Er, yes Mum,' said Art, patting his suitcase with his hand.

'What about your sports bag?' Asked Mrs Myatt.

'I've put it in the hallway Mum.'

'Ok, I'll go and check the house.'

His mother was very security conscious always making sure her house was secure before leaving to go somewhere. She walked back downstairs into the sitting room and started to switch off and unplug electrical items. She then continued walking around the rest of the house checking windows, switching off and unplugging anything she could find.

Art stayed in his bedroom sitting on his bed thinking about Mr Beagle. He smiled to himself as he pictured Mr Beagle at his Aunt Hayley's cottage with his brown and white markings, large ears flapping up and down and tail wagging like a propeller as he danced excitedly around the kitchen.

He was tempted to ask the Traveller's Map for Mr Beagle's location but he knew his mother was getting ready to leave. Art couldn't wait and just wanted to know that Mr Beagle was safe. He removed the map from his pocket and carefully unwrapped it. He then quietly asked it to show him Mr Beagle's location. He waited and waited as the map flickered, but no information or picture was shown to help him locate Mr Beagle.

He continued staring at the map until he was startled by the sound of footsteps as his mother walked into his bedroom. He turned and looked at her still holding the map in his hands out in front of him. She looked at the Art holding the map with a puzzled look on her face.

'Art, why are you staring at a piece of blank paper?' She asked. 'Are you ready to leave?'

'Er, yes Mum,' said Art, quickly folding the map back up.

'Hurry then, let's get going,' she said. 'Please make sure you check your window and plugs, before leaving your room.'

His mother walked out of his bedroom and down the stairs. She waited for Art in the hallway. Several seconds passed before Mrs Myatt became impatient and decided to go and take Art's sports bag to her car. When she got to the car she unlocked it and opened the boot placing his bag inside. Mrs Myatt left the boot open ready for Art's suitcase. As she started to walk back to the house a beautiful array of green and yellow lights cascaded from the sky into the boot. The array of colours lasted only for seconds before disappearing in a flash back up into the sky. Mrs Myatt was completely unaware of the lights as she entered her house. She waited patiently at the bottom of the stairs hoping Art would soon be ready to leave.

Art, still in his bedroom, put the map back in his

pocket wondering why the map didn't help him. He checked his window, switched off the plugs as his mother asked, before lifting his suitcase from the bed and walking downstairs into the hallway.

'I think the house is safe and secure Art. Shall we go?'

'Er, yes,' said Art, walking towards the front door.

He opened the front door for his mother and lifted his suitcase from the house out onto the driveway. Art waited by his suitcase as his mother set the security alarm and closed the front door. They both walked to the car and Art used all of his strength to load his suitcase into the boot of the car. His mother closed the boot and soon afterwards they drove off heading to the village of Brillion.

As the car moved Art was in deep thought about Mr Beagle. He really hoped Mr Beagle was safe and not involved in any new trouble or mischief.

To occupy his mind he decided to read his rugby magazine again, hoping the journey to Brillion wouldn't take too long.

His mother noticed Art was quiet so to break the silence she decided to turn the radio on and listen to music being played by the local Oxfordshire radio station "Snap FM". As they travelled, the Snap FM presenter advertised the fun weekend at Brillion. This pleased Art and helped him to stop thinking about Mr Beagle for a short while.

They continued their journey along the country roads through Oxfordshire passing beautiful countryside scenery and amazing architecture of properties in country villages.

As they approached Brillion there were cyclists

peddling fast in groups along the road in front of them slowing the cars right down. Art looked out of the window noticing banners advertising the fun weekend. He could also see people walking around in different costume designs, carrying leaflets and bunches of coloured balloons. Gradually, they continued into Brillion and towards the village green where they could see a large blue marquee tent in the middle. Outside the marquee was a very big advertisement sign.

MARLOCK'S MARQUEE OF WONDERS

INVITES YOU TO COME AND SEE

CHARLIE THE CLOWN

AND OUR

STAR ATTRACTION:

MARLOCK THE MAGICIAN

Art stared at the sign as his mother drove past the marquee hoping he would get a chance to go and visit the marquee before leaving Brillion.

When they arrived at Hayley's cottage Art opened his door and climbed out of the car onto the payment. He looked at the cottage remembering the last time he stayed.

'Art, help me with your suitcase please,' his mother said, as she opened the boot.

As the boot lifted upwards a small creature jumped out of the boot down onto the road and scrambled under the car. Mrs Myatt was completely unaware of the creature as she stepped backwards away from the car.

Art smiled at his mother as he walked to the back of the car. Next he then carefully lent over and looked inside the boot. He gripped his suitcase tightly with both of his hands before lifting it out and placing it on the path in front of Hayley's cottage. He then lifted his sports bag out, placing it next to his suitcase. Art waited by his luggage watching as his mother closed the boot and walked around the car making sure it was locked. As he waited he noticed something moving under the car. He crouched down, pressing his hands on the ground to look under the car.

'Art, have you lost something?' Asked his mother.

Art quickly got back up and rubbed his hands together to remove the dust.

'Er, no mum, just thought I saw something,' he said, rubbing his head with his hand.

Mrs Myatt smiled at him as she picked up his sports bag.

'You've got some dirt on your forehead Art,' she said, staring at his head. 'Come on let's go and see your Aunt Hayley.'

The little creature quickly ran from underneath the car and jumped onto the side of Art's suitcase, clinging tightly with its claws and hiding from sight. Mrs Myatt walked slowly down the path towards the cottage with Art following, urgently trying to remove the dirt from his forehead. As they arrived outside the large wooden door to the cottage, it opened wide in front of them. Standing in the doorway was Hayley. A lovely smell of home cooking soon floated out past Hayley, through

the open door and past Mrs Myatt, finally stopping at
Art. His nose twitched as the aroma from the cooking
engulfed him. He was in food heaven. He knew his
Aunt Hayley had been cooking and that it meant
plenty of chocolate goodies. Hayley smiled first at Mrs
Myatt, then at Art, before inviting them both inside
her cottage.

'How long has Mr Beagle been missing Aunt
Hayley?' Art asked.

'Since very early this morning Art. I let him in the
back garden and I haven't seen him since. He's been
acting very strange recently, not his normal self. He
has stayed close to the cottage, acting very alert and is
always behind me. It's like he's worried about
something.'

'Don't worry sister, I'm sure he's not gone far,' said
Mrs Myatt trying to comfort her.

Hayley paused for a moment, smiled and nodded in
agreement before offering her guests something to eat
and drink. Mrs Myatt and Art sat in the kitchen
enjoying the wonderful taste of Hayley's baking. Art
wanted to open the Traveller's Map again to find Mr
Beagle but he knew he needed to wait until he was on
his own or with Amy.

Hayley placed a large plate of chocolate cookies on
the worktop near to where Art was sitting. As he
reached to take one, someone knocked very loudly on
the wooden door to the cottage making him drop the
cookie back onto the plate.

CHAPTER TWO

THE LITTLE GREEN DRAGON

Hayley walked to the door and opened it. Standing outside with Mr Beagle at her side was Amy. Hayley was pleased to see Amy with Mr Beagle but before she could do or say anything else, Mr Beagle lifted himself up from the ground, raised his body high and started to wag his tail fast.

He sensed Art was sitting in the kitchen and he wanted to go and see him.

Hayley and Amy watched as Mr Beagle walked into the cottage, past Hayley's legs, then started to run in search of Art.

Hayley was relieved to see Mr Beagle again. She invited Amy inside her cottage and closed the door behind her.

As Mr Beagle approached Art, he tried to slow down and stop but instead he slid along the shiny floor crashing into Art's sports bag lying on the ground. The sports bag moved along the floor crashing into Art's suitcase. The creature, a Little Green Dragon still attached to Art's suitcase, hissed in disapproval at Mr Beagle.

Mr Beagle looked at the Little Green Dragon as he tried to compose himself.

Everyone else in the kitchen was unaware of the Little Green Dragon as it clung tightly to Art's suitcase, hidden - watching Mr Beagle carefully.

Art laughed as Mr Beagle continued to try and compose himself. Mr Beagle looked at Art and started to nudge his legs with his head.

'Hello Mr Beagle,' said Art, ruffling his head and ears gently with his hands. 'I've missed you.'

Mr Beagle enjoyed all the fuss and Art was very pleased to see him again. Hayley and Mrs Myatt looked on, smiling at Art with Mr Beagle.

Amy stood in the kitchen next to Hayley wondering when Art would notice her. She put her hand over her mouth and coughed loudly before walking nearer to Art.

'Hello Art,' she said, smiling.

Art stopped ruffling Mr Beagle's ears and looked at Amy. He felt his face go warm as his cheeks went bright red. Mrs Myatt and Hayley smiled at them both as Art quickly got up from the chair to talk to Amy.

Mr Beagle rested on the ground next to them, at the same time keeping a close watch on the Little Green Dragon.

'Er - Sorry Amy I didn't know you were there…I mean…in the kitchen,' Art mumbled.

'That's ok Art, nice to see you again,' said Amy, turning to face Hayley.

'I found Mr Beagle wandering on the village green near to that big blue tent Hayley,' said Amy, looking puzzled. 'I decided to bring him back to you.'

'Yes, thank you Amy,' said Hayley, looking at Mr Beagle. 'I've been worried about him.'

Mr Beagle sat quietly on the floor resting with his legs stretched fully out and his ears flopped down over his head - still focusing on the Little Green Dragon.

'Can I take Art for a walk into the village please Mrs Myatt?' Amy asked.

'Yes, that should be ok, but you need to take your suitcase and sports bag upstairs first Art,' said Mrs Myatt, glancing at her sister.

'Yes, that's ok; you're in the same bedroom as before Art. The one that looks out onto the back garden,' said Hayley, smiling at him.

'Thanks Aunt Hayley,' said Art, quickly lifting his suitcase up from the floor. 'I'll come back down and get my sports bag.'

'I'll bring your sports bag for you,' said Amy, as she grabbed its handles.

Hayley and Mrs Myatt smiled as Art and Amy both left the room with Mr Beagle following close behind. Mr Beagle kept a careful watch on the Little Green Dragon still hiding but clinging tightly to Art's suitcase. As Art approached his bedroom Mr Beagle barked gently making Amy jump.

Art shook his head and ignored Mr Beagle. He entered the bedroom and carefully laid his suitcase on the end of his bed, completely unaware of the Little Green Dragon attached to his suitcase. Amy handed him his sports bag and he placed it on the bed next to the suitcase.

The room smelt a little stuffy so Art decided to open the window to let in some air.

Mr Beagle was standing just inside the doorway with Amy. Art walked towards Amy and Mr Beagle. As he approached them Mr Beagle looked up at Art and barked again but this time a little bit louder.

'What's the matter Mr Beagle?' said Art, looking at him.

'I think he's trying to tell you something Art,' Amy said.

While they were both looking at Mr Beagle, the Little Green Dragon hopped off the suitcase and ran, hiding under Art's pillows.

Mr Beagle walked towards Art's bed moving his head from side to side sniffing in search of the Little Green Dragon. He then jumped up onto the bed to continue his search.

'Mr Beagle, come on,' Amy said. 'We need to go.'

Mr Beagle ignored Amy and carefully moved closer to the suitcase sniffing loudly.

'Come on Mr Beagle, we're going,' said Art, as they both waited by the bedroom door for him, ready to leave.

Mr Beagle ignored both Art and Amy. He sensed the Little Green Dragon had moved from the suitcase to hide. He moved from the suitcase in the direction of the pillows so quickly, that he caught his paws on the bed sheets, making him trip and fall forwards. Mr Beagle crashed headfirst into the pillows making the Little Green Dragon hiss at him before flying from the bed in the direction of where Art and Amy were standing.

Art and Amy stared in disbelief at the Little Green

Dragon as it flapped its little wings landing safely on the floor in front of them. With the exception of yellow markings on its head and on the tips of its wings and at the end of its claws, it was green in colour. It had a small spiky head, pointed sharp white teeth, bright yellow eyes and a long tail. The Little Green Dragon opened its mouth slightly and walked towards Art and Amy - it's tail swishing from side to side as it moved.

Meanwhile Mr Beagle was still trying to untangle his claws from the bed sheets. He could see the Little Green Dragon, but could do nothing to help.

The Little Green Dragon's claws tapped the bedroom floor as it stopped in front of Art and Amy. It moved its head from side to side as it looked up at them.

Art and Amy looked at each other both wondering what to do next.

Mr Beagle finally untangled himself and very gently jumped down from the bed and sat on the floor near the Little Green Dragon…but not too close.

The Little Green Dragon looked at Mr Beagle, raised its wings wide and opened its mouth to try and communicate with him. Instead, a puff of smoke came out of its nose as small coloured flames flew out of its mouth just catching the end of Mr Beagle's tail.

Mr Beagle jumped and moved his tail away. He licked the end of his tail to cool it down.
Art and Amy were speechless as they watched the Little Green Dragon close its wings and step backwards away from Mr Beagle. The Little Green Dragon was confused. He knew he should be home in Dragon Valley but instead he was in a strange place he

didn't know.

CHAPTER THREE

FLIGHT OF THE DRAGON

The Little Green Dragon opened its wings wide and gave them a little flap. It then glanced at Art, Amy and Mr Beagle, before a little bit more smoke came out of its nose.

Mr Beagle moved backwards hiding his tail.

The Little Green Dragon made a noise then flapped its wings again slowly lifting itself from the ground into the air and eventually landing on the end of Art's bed. It rested for several seconds before opening its wings again to fly from the bed in the direction of the open window. It hovered in the air before landing unsteadily on the windowsill. The Little Green Dragon wobbled as it looked around at Art and Amy one more time before lifting itself off the windowsill and flying through the open window out towards the garden.

Art and Amy rushed to the window and watched as the Little Green Dragon flapped its little wings struggling to fly across the gardens at the back of the cottages. As the Little Green Dragon flew it bobbed up and down in the wind trying to keep itself steady.

Mr Beagle rushed across to Art and Amy and barked making them both jump. They tried to ignore Mr Beagle for a moment while they watched the Little Green Dragon fly to the end of the cottages and out of sight.

'Was that a Little Green Dragon Amy?' Art asked.

'Yes, I think so,' said Amy hesitantly.

Mr Beagle barked again, trying to attract their attention.

Art and Amy turned around to look at Mr Beagle. They could both tell by the look on Mr Beagle's face that he wanted to go and find the Little Green Dragon.

'Ok, Mr Beagle,' said Art. 'Let's go and find your little friend.'

'Do you think we should tell your mum or Hayley first,' Amy said.

'Tell them what? We just saw a Little Green Dragon and it flew out of the window. No, let's go for a walk and see if we can find it.'

Amy felt uneasy but she agreed to go and search for the Little Green Dragon.

Mr Beagle barked again in agreement.

'Yes, ok Mr Beagle, let's go,' Art said.

Mr Beagle lifted his ears up ready to go for a walk and to find the Little Green Dragon.

Art closed his window and they all left his bedroom and walked back downstairs into the hallway.

'We're just going mum,' Art shouted.

'Ok, see you later,' she said. 'Have fun!'

Mr Beagle was eager to leave the cottage. As Art

opened the cottage door he ran in front of Art and Amy, continuing down to the end of the cottage path leaving them both behind.

Art looked at Mr Beagle and smiled to himself.

Mr Beagle waited for Art and Amy to catch him up before the three of them left the cottage in search of the Little Green Dragon.

As Art and Amy walked slowly past the cottages, they looked up into the beautiful blue sky for any sign of the Little Green Dragon. Mr Beagle walked in front of them with his tail upright and his ears bobbing up and down. He was also searching for the Little Green Dragon but used his nose instead, to try and find any scent left behind. When they reached the end of the cottages, Amy thought she caught a glimpse of the Little Green Dragon flying over towards the blue marquee tent situated on the village green.

After a brief discussion they decided to go and see what they could find. Mr Beagle continued to walk in front of them moving his head from side to side sniffing the ground as he walked. Amy was particularly eager to explain to Art about the summer fun weekend in Brillion. She knew Art was a keen rugby player and wanted to make him aware of Brillion's sport's event taking place on Saturday afternoon in the village sports field where people could win certificates and a trophy. They talked as they walked and Amy explained to Art about the sports event. Art had packed his sports kit before he left his home and was keen to enter one or more of the competitions.

As they approached the village green they could see the big blue marquee tent. It was unusual in design with pointed shaped corners and golden coloured poles supporting each segment. On top of the marquee were wonderful coloured drawings of different animals that reflected in the sunshine. In the middle of the marquee was a very tall pole, which reached out through the top of the marquee, high up into the sky.

They continued walking towards the marquee. Standing outside by the advertisement sign was a tall thin man, wearing a tall black hat, dark black suit, white shirt, black tie and shiny black shoes. Next to him sitting on the ground was a large white dog with piercing black eyes. Mr Beagle barked at the dog and left Art and Amy behind as he ran fast towards the other dog. The other dog lifted its huge body from the ground and walked slowly forwards waiting for Mr Beagle to arrive.

CHAPTER FOUR

MISSING

Back at 'Honeypot Cottage' Hayley and Mrs Myatt were getting ready to pop down to the village and arrange some special chocolates for Hayley's shop window display. They finished packing all the chocolates and display items and left the cottage. Mrs Myatt offered to drive them into the village but Hayley wanted to walk. They had only walked for a short distance carrying all of the items when Hayley started to feel tired and wished she had taken her sister's offer up to drive them to her shop.

When they arrived, they were met by a very distressed looking Farmer Calloway.

'Someone's taken my Basset Hound,' he said, looking upset. 'Can I ask you if I can put this poster in your window please Hayley?'

'Yes of course you can Mr Calloway. Do you know when your dog went missing?' Hayley asked.

'Last night,' he said. 'He was in the yard and there were all these lights in the sky then he just vanished. I've looked everywhere for him. It's not like him, he's very loyal,' said Farmer Calloway wiping tears from his eyes.

Mrs Myatt felt sad for Farmer Calloway and tried to comfort him by explaining she would ask her son Art to look out for him.

'Thank you,' he said, before handing Hayley the poster of his Basset Hound.

'I must be going now,' he said. 'I need to go back to my farm and feed my sheep.'

Farmer Calloway walked away looking from side to side for any sign of his missing dog.

Before Hayley arranged her display she placed the poster in her window. Mrs Myatt went outside to look at it.

'Oh look, Hayley,' she said. 'He's so cute. Big floppy ears and…' Mrs Myatt stopped talking. She remembered reading an article in a local paper recently about sightings of bright lights at night in the sky above Oxfordshire and sudden disappearances of certain breeds of animals.

'Hayley, I think I've read something about this,' she said, walking back into the shop.

'What is it?' Hayley asked.

'In a local paper recently a reporter wrote an article about reporting's of bright lights at night in the sky above Oxfordshire and then the sudden disappearances of certain breeds of animals,' Mrs Myatt said.

'Have you still got the paper at home?' Hayley asked.

'Not sure, but I'll check when I get back later,' Mrs Myatt said.

'Strange lights in the sky at night, isn't it exciting,' said Hayley, moving chocolate displays around in her shop window.

'Hayley, what about the animals?' Mrs Myatt said.

'Yes, sorry, of course, it's just exciting sister, bright lights at night,' Hayley said. 'Seriously though, I do hope Farmer Calloway finds his Basset Hound.'

Hayley and Mrs Myatt finished off arranging the window display. Hayley was keen to show her sister the location where the village had plans to hold a Midsummer Night's Ball. It was only a short walk from her shop and easy to find because signs were displayed on most of the outside walls of properties in the middle of the village, giving directions to all of the Brillion's events for the weekend.

When they arrived, Mrs Myatt was mesmerized by the sight of a very large, open design building. It was pure white, with a layered canopy above and supported by steel upright posts. It was decorated inside and out with lights, flowers, balloons and confetti of all different shapes and colours.

'Wow,' said Mrs Myatt, 'it's beautiful Hayley.'

'Yes, I know, everyone here in Brillion has worked very hard to decorate it,' Hayley said. 'There's a local band coming to play live soft music and there will be food for when everyone gets hungry. It should be fun…'

Hayley and Mrs Myatt were interrupted by the sound of someone testing a loud speaker.

'123, 123, testing, testing, 123, 123, testing,' a man's squeaky voice said.

'Oh dear. It's Mr Popkiss. Come on let's go back to my cottage. I'll show you a shorter route,' said Hayley, chuckling to herself.

They both started to walk slowly back to Hayley's cottage talking excitably about Brillion's fun weekend. As they walked they heard someone shouting.

'Tibbles! Where are you Tibbles?' A lady's voice said.

As Hayley and Mrs Myatt approached the lady she stopped them and asked if they had seen her Shiz-tzu dog, Tibbles. They listened as the lady told them how she saw bright lights in the sky, then when she let her dog out in the garden, soon afterwards her dog went missing. The same night as Farmer Calloway's Basset Hound went missing.

Hayley and Mrs Myatt suggested to the lady she should tell the Police about the bright lights in the sky and the disappearance of Tibbles. Before continuing their walk back to the cottage they wished her all the best in finding Tibbles.

'What do you think is going on Hayley,' Mrs Myatt said.

'I don't know, but I'm not letting Mr Beagle out again at night unless I'm with him. I couldn't face being without him,' said Hayley seriously.

'Perhaps there's a logical reason for the dogs going missing Hayley. When I go back home later, I'll search for the newspaper to see if there's something I missed,' said Mrs Myatt trying to comfort her sister. 'Anyway, Art will look after you and Mr Beagle. He's really strong for his age; he plays rugby for the county now. I'm really proud of him.'

'Yes, I know sister, he's a good boy and I know

he'll do his best to look after us all and Mr Beagle,'
Hayley said.

When they arrived back at the cottage Hayley and
Mrs Myatt rested and drank tea and ate biscuits while
they waited for Art, Amy and Mr Beagle to return.

CHAPTER FIVE

MARLOCK THE MAGICIAN

Art and Amy walked faster trying to catch up with Mr Beagle. Before they could do anything else, Mr Beagle reached the other dog and stopped just in front of him. The other dog was much larger and taller than Mr Beagle. He walked slightly forwards and looked down at Mr Beagle with his piercing black eyes. Art and Amy were really worried for Mr Beagle's safety. They ran as fast as they could and stopped close to Mr Beagle. They both tried to encourage Mr Beagle to move away from the other dog but he ignored them. The tall, thin man looked on saying nothing. Mr Beagle continued to ignore Art and Amy; he was focused, his back was raised and his tail upright and he knew what he wanted to do. Art and Amy were helpless and unsure of what to do next.

They watched as Mr Beagle first started to move his tail slowly from side to side and move forwards closer to the other dog. The other dog also moved forward, his body towering over Mr Beagle. In response, Mr Beagle wagged his tail really fast in excitement and the other dog moved his head down closer to Mr Beagle, to greet him.

Art and Amy were relieved. They looked on as Mr Beagle played happily with the other dog, just as if he had known him for years.

'Wonder how Mr Beagle knows this dog, Amy?' Art asked.

'I don't know, but I did find him wandering around here earlier,' said Amy smiling. 'Perhaps he's his new friend?'

The tall, thin man walked forward towards Art and Amy, removed his hat and bowed down slightly.

'Good afternoon, my name is Marlock and that is my dog, Star,' he said, standing up and putting his hat back on his head. 'You don't need to worry, Star and Mr Beagle are old friends from a different time and place.'

'Oh, hello, my name is Art Myatt and this is my friend Amy,' said Art politely.

'Oh yes, I've been expecting you,' Marlock said smiling.

They all watched as Mr Beagle and Star moved away and sat on the grass next to each other peacefully. They made noises as if they were speaking to each other.

'Sorry, did you say, expecting us, what do you mean?' asked Amy feeling slightly concerned.

'The famous Art Myatt with Amy and Mr Beagle. You are very well known. Have you seen Samuel recently?'

'Do you know Samuel?' asked Art, unaware of Amy's concerns.

'Yes, of course, we go back a long way,' said Marlock. 'You could say I've been an admirer of Samuel's magic for years.'

'I didn't know he was a magician,' Amy said.

'Mm, well a kind of magician I suppose. Anyway, it doesn't matter, do you both want to come and see us in our special opening event tomorrow afternoon?' Marlock asked.

'Yes, please,' said Art, without thinking.

'Are you sure we will have time Art?' Asked Amy, raising her eyebrows and looking seriously at him.

'Er-yes, why not,' said Art. 'It should be fun.'

'Good,' said Marlock, putting his hand in his jacket pocket. 'Here are two very special front seat tickets for our opening event at 2.30pm,' he said, handing the tickets to Art. 'See you tomorrow.'

'Ok,' Art said.

'Come now, Star,' said Marlock loudly, turning to walk back towards the entrance to the marquee.

Star raised his body from the ground and made one final noise to Mr Beagle before following Marlock back towards the marquee and through the entrance to go inside. The canvas doors to the marquee closed tightly behind them securing the entrance.

'Art why did you say we would go tomorrow,' Amy said.

'Er…I thought you would like to go,' Art replied.

Mr Beagle got up from the ground, walked over to the marquee tent. He was pleased to see his old friend again but he sensed something was going to happen soon and that his friend might be in danger. He sat down outside the entrance, making noises and feeling sad.

'See, even Mr Beagle thinks something's wrong Art. I'm worried,' said Amy, unaware of Mr Beagle's true feelings.

'Oh, come on Amy it's the opening event, what could possibly go wrong! Let's go and look at the sports field,' said Art, holding the tickets in his hand.

Amy sighed. She had a bad feeling about Marlock, the marquee and the opening event.

Mr Beagle continued to sit outside the marquee entrance. Art walked over to him to comfort him. Eventually Mr Beagle moved away from the marquee and walked with Art across to Amy.

'Shall we go to the sports field Mr Beagle?' said Amy smiling at him. 'Come on let's go,' she said, urgently walking away from the marquee.

Art followed but he walked slowly with Mr Beagle still looking for any sign of the Little Green Dragon.

'Come on Art, catch up,' Amy said laughing.

Art slowed his pace even more as he continued to look around at the surroundings for any sign of the Little Green Dragon. As he walked he remembered the Traveller's Map and quickly searched his trousers pocket for the map. He found it and carefully took it out of his pocket to unwrap it. He then asked the map to show him the location of the Little Green Dragon. This time the map didn't take very long at all to show Art a picture. But the picture made Art gasp with surprise. It was not what he expected to see.

CHAPTER SIX

IN SAFE HANDS

'Amy stop! You need to see this,' Art said loudly.

Amy rushed back to where Art was standing. He held the map out in front of him for Amy to see.

'I was right Art,' she said pointing at the map. 'I knew there was something strange about Marlock and…that marquee. Look, the map is all cloudy but I think there's lots of strange looking…creatures in cages. It's difficult to see but it looks really weird if you ask me.'

'Yes, I know Amy, but where is the Little Green Dragon?' said Art, staring at the map.

Mr Beagle barked trying to attract Art's attention.

'Not now Mr Beagle,' said Art, trying to concentrate.

Mr Beagle nudged Art's legs with his head. He barked again, he then looked up at the very tall pole coming out of the middle of the marquee. Sitting on top in the sunshine was the Little Green Dragon.

'Look Art,' said Amy pointing at the top of the pole. 'The Little Green Dragon. He's there, sitting on top of the pole.'

Art stopped looking at the map and looked up at the pole. Sure enough it was the Little Green Dragon. The Dragon noticed Art and Amy looking at him. He wobbled a little and gripped the pole tightly with his claws, then he opened his wings preparing for another flight.

'Looks like he's going somewhere again Amy,' Art said.

'He needs to hurry up,' said Amy. 'Look there's some people climbing out from the top of the marquee up the pole towards him and…they've got a net or something'

Art looked and sure enough he could see four people climbing steadily up the pole carrying nets. Each one moved one after another. Their bodies and faces were completely covered from sight with blue cloth just as if they came from outer space and didn't want to be recognized.

'Any ideas Mr Beagle?' Art said.

Mr Beagle barked and stepped slightly away from Art and Amy. He looked at the Little Green Dragon before raising his head high and letting out a very loud and long howl. This was followed by several seconds of urgent barking.

On hearing this the Little Green Dragon flapped his little wings, lifted himself off the top of the pole and started to fly. One of the people climbing the pole immediately threw a net in the direction of the Little Green Dragon to catch him. Art and Amy watched as the Little Green Dragon tried to dodge the net. As it opened, it caught the end of the Little Green Dragon's wing, knocking him off balance. The Little Green Dragon spun out of control, falling downwards towards the marquee.

The four people hung onto the pole tightly before starting to climb back down the pole to wait for the Little Green Dragon and to finally catch him in their nets.

Mr Beagle looked up at the Little Green Dragon and barked again and again trying to get him to open his wings and fly.

Amy shouted and shouted to The Little Green Dragon. 'Flap your wings Little Green Dragon.'

The Little Green Dragon heard Mr Beagle and Amy call to him and in desperation he tried to compose itself. He was getting closer to the marquee and the four people from the marquee were waiting for him with their nets. The Little Green Dragon was getting tired but he tried one last time to fly. He used all of his strength to compose himself and gave his wings a strong flap. Before he knew it, he was flying again.

'Well done Little Green Dragon,' Amy shouted loudly.

Mr Beagle barked in approval.

This gave the Little Green Dragon encouragement. He flapped his wings to move himself away from the marquee. As his glided away, more nets were thrown at him. The people from the marquee still hoped to catch him. In a panic the Little Green Dragon flapped his wings harder than he had ever done before moving himself away from the nets and over to near where Art was standing.

Art watched as the Little Green Dragon glided high in the air. He continued watching and soon realized the Little Green Dragon was in trouble. The Little Green Dragon started to slow down. He was exhausted and he was struggling to stay in the air. He hovered, trying to use the wind to help him stay in one position.

Without thinking Art moved quickly from where he was standing and rushed over to stand under where the Little Green Dragon was hovering.

He called out to the Little Green Dragon. 'You'll be safe with me Little Green Dragon. I'll look after you.'

Art stretched his arms out in front of him and opened up his hands wide.

Amy watched as the Little Green Dragon looked down at Art before lowering himself downwards towards his hands. He landed very gently in Art's hands and closed his wings.

'There you go Little Green Dragon,' said Art, smiling at him.

The Little Green Dragon looked at Art. He was very tired and was struggling to keep his eyes open. He opened his mouth making squeaking noises at Art. Art smiled at the Little Green Dragon and pulled his arms in closer to his body.

'I didn't know you could be so soppy Art,' said Amy teasing him.

'Er…yes, I mean no,' said Art, still admiring the Little Green Dragon.

'Well done Art for your quick thinking; I'm very proud of you,' Amy said.

Art smiled at Amy and he felt his face go warm and his cheeks soon went red. He was feeling just slightly embarrassed. They both looked at the Little Green Dragon sitting comfortably in Art's hands.

Mr Beagle arrived and gave a gentle bark of approval.

A little puff of smoke came out of the Little Green Dragon's nose as he started to fall fast asleep.

CHAPTER SEVEN

A HUNGRY DRAGON

'Art look, there are people marching towards us from the marquee,' said Amy, looking worried.

Mr Beagle raised his body, then lifted his tail and growled loudly.

Art turned around to see Marlock walking towards him with the same four people who climbed up the pole to catch the Little Green Dragon.

Mr Beagle walked slightly away from Art and Amy and forwards to meet Marlock and his people. Mr Beagle growled again but this time showing his teeth.

'We should go Art,' Amy said.

Art held the Little Green Dragon close to his body trying to hide him under his jacket.

Marlock and his people stopped a short distance away from Mr Beagle.

'Come now Mr Beagle, you know who I am, why do you growl at me?' Marlock said.

Mr Beagle was having none of it. He walked closer to Marlock, raised his head high and he let out a very high pitched howling noise. The noise had no effect on Marlock, Art or Amy but the people with Marlock soon found the noise uncomfortable and placed their hands over their cloth covered ears to try and block out the noise. Mr Beagle continued howling and raised the noise to a higher level. It was too much for Marlock's people. They mumbled to Marlock before running as fast as they could back to the marquee.

Mr Beagle stopped howling but stayed in the same spot keeping a very close eye on Marlock.

'Well Mr Beagle, Samuel would be very proud of you,' Marlock said.

Mr Beagle barked once to acknowledge Marlock before moving back towards Art and Amy.

'What is it you want Marlock?' Art asked.

'Nothing really Art, I just wanted to say sorry for any distress my people may have caused the Little Green Dragon.'

Art looked at the Little Green Dragon. He was fast asleep in his hands, unaware of Marlock.

'That's ok, we need to go now,' Art said. 'Come on Mr Beagle.'

'He is very special you know; very special indeed. We could look after him for you, if you like Art?' Marlock said.

'What, like those creatures you've got locked in cages,' Amy snapped.

'Oh, I see, you know…they're not prisoners; we keep them in cages for protection. Those creatures are not from around here and could be dangerous to the people of Brillion. You might get the opportunity to see them all at our special opening show tomorrow. So, before I go, would you like me to take care of the Little Green Dragon? I know what to feed him.'

Mr Beagle immediately growled to show his disapproval.

'Ok, Mr Beagle. You win. Still another time I suppose, until tomorrow then Art?' said Marlock, before starting to walk back to the Marquee.

'What a strange person Art. I'm really not sure about him. Does he really know Samuel?' Amy said.

'Mm…he is strange and he seems to know about us and Mr Beagle,' Art said. 'Come on, let's get this little chap somewhere safe.'

Art moved the Little Green Dragon closer to his body. The Little Green Dragon woke slightly and climbed from Art's hands under his jacket and into a large deep pocket.

'But to where Art? How do you look after a Dragon?' said Amy, looking worried.

'Don't know, but I'm sure we'll think of something. Let's go and find somewhere to sit for a while so we can work out what to do.'

'Ok, let's go and sit on the bench over there,' said Amy, pointing at a wooden bench at the edge of the village green.

Art checked that the Little Green Dragon was safe and they walked quickly towards the bench. Mr Beagle ran in front of them, sniffing the ground searching for something. As Art and Amy arrived at the bench, Mr Beagle disappeared into an overgrown mass of brightly green plants and grass at the edge of the village green. Art and Amy looked but all they could see was the top of his tail sticking out of the top and moving as he walked.

'What's Mr Beagle doing?' Amy asked.

Just at that same moment Mr Beagle sprung out from the overgrown mass, carrying a very strange-looking green plant, with bright yellow leaves in his mouth.

'Looks like we're going to find out very soon,' Art said. 'He's found something...and it's very long and green and yellow?'

They both stared at Mr Beagle running towards them happily carrying the plant. The leaves from the plant hung down to the ground covering the front of his legs. He stopped just in front of Art, dropping the plant on the ground next to his shoes.

Mr Beagle looked up at Art and barked.

Art looked very puzzled, wondering what to do next.

Mr Beagle nudged the plant with his nose onto Art's right shoe. He then walked backwards and wagged his tail very fast, gently barking at Art again.

'I think he wants you to pick that...plant up Art,' said Amy chuckling.

Art felt the Little Green Dragon move inside his pocket.

'Ok,' said Art, looking down at the plant.

Art lent forwards trying not to disturb the Little Green Dragon and stretched his arm out to pick the plant up.

Amy laughed as Art tried to pick it up with his fingers. It was too big and dropped back down onto his shoe.

'Grab it with your hand Art. It won't bite,' said Amy, teasing him.

Art felt his face go warm as he grabbed the plant with his hand and lifted it up onto his lap. The leaves from the plant hung down over his legs towards the ground. He quickly rubbed his hands together to remove dirt.

Mr Beagle barked again waking the Little Green Dragon.

Art felt the Little Green Dragon move in his pocket.

Mr Beagle barked again but this time a little louder.

The Little Green Dragon climbed out of Art's jacket pocket and out down onto his lap.

Mr Beagle wagged his tail very fast watching as the Little Green Dragon nibbled one of the leaves from the plant.

'Look Art, Mr Beagle's found him something to eat,' Amy said. 'He looks like he's enjoying it and he's really hungry.'

Art felt slightly uncomfortable as the Little Green Dragon started to tuck into more of the plant. This carried on for several minutes until the Little Green Dragon finished eating all of the plant. He then carefully walked across Art's lap towards his knees. He stopped and wobbled slightly but then he opened his wings out and stretched them fully open. A little bit of smoke came out of his nose at the same time making Art feel worried.

On seeing the smoke, Mr Beagle moved backwards away from the bench, hiding his tail.

Amy smiled as she watched the Little Green Dragon stretch himself before settling down happily on Art's lap.

'Er-I think we should go back soon,' said Art,

keeping a very close eye on the Little Green Dragon.

'Yes, I agree, looks like you've made a friend Art,' said Amy, chuckling to herself. 'Are you going to carry the Little Green Dragon?'

'Er-I suppose so,' Art said.

Art carefully put his hands around the Little Green Dragon to carry him. He lifted the Little Green Dragon up close to his body and got up from the bench. The Little Green Dragon, now a little bit heavier from eating the plant, scrambled from Art's hands, up under his jacket and back into Art's pocket making the jacket sag slightly on one side.

'Art, where are you going to keep the Little Green Dragon?' Amy asked.

'Er, not sure yet, probably in my bedroom somewhere?'

'That should be interesting,' Amy said.

Mr Beagle walked over to Art's side, looked up at him and barked gently.

Art looked at Mr Beagle and smiled.

'We had better get going Art,' said Amy, smiling at him.

'Ok, come on Mr Beagle,' said Art, supporting his jacket with his hand.

As they started to walk from the village green back to the cottages, Amy was deep in thought. Suddenly she stopped and grabbed Art's arm.

'I've been thinking Art, how about giving the Little Green Dragon a name?'

'Er-Yes, I suppose so. What do you suggest?' Art said.

Amy paused for a moment. Then she remembered the Little Green Dragon's spiky head.

43

'How about Spiky,' Amy said.

'Mm…Spiky. Yes, sounds good to me,' Art said. 'Spiky it is.'

CHAPTER EIGHT

MESSAGE IN A BOX

They arrived back outside 'Honeypot Cottage' to find a parcel delivery van parked outside Hayley's cottage. The driver's door was wide open and they could hear the local Snap FM radio presenter playing music. Next, the driver of the van, a tall man wearing a blue shirt and black trousers, walked away from the cottage, down the path and through the gate. He smiled at Art and Amy before getting into his van and driving away.

'Wonder what he delivered,' Amy said.

'Probably another collar for Mr Beagle,' Art joked.

Mr Beagle made a groaning noise and sat down on the ground next to Art.

'Now, now, Mr Beagle, you look very nice in your bright blue collar,' Amy said smiling.

'I suppose I had better go now Art,' Amy said. 'The opening event for Brillion's fun weekend is on the sports field at 6pm. All of the roads are being closed for two hours so people can walk around the village safely to look at stalls and things. Shall I call for you, say, at 5:30 pm?'

'Yes, ok Amy, that would be great. See you later then,' said Art, still supporting the side of the jacket where Spiky was sleeping in his pocket.

Art waited for Amy to walk along the path at the front of the cottages and then safely down the path to her cottage before starting the short walk to Hayley's. He looked behind him to find Mr Beagle still making his way up the cottage path.

'Come on Mr Beagle, I was only joking about the collar,' Art said.

Art waited for Mr Beagle to reach him. He then checked his jacket pocket making sure Spiky was sleeping before knocking on the cottage door. The door opened quickly and standing inside to greet them was Hayley.

'Do come in Art, there's a parcel inside for you,' said Hayley excited.

'A parcel, I'm not expecting any parcels,' Art said.

'It's addressed to you,' Hayley said. 'I've put it in your bedroom for you.'

'Er…Thanks Aunt Hayley, I'll go upstairs and look at it,' Art said.

'It's 4pm and I think you mother is nearly ready to leave Art. Perhaps you should go and see her first?' Hayley said.

Art nodded in acknowledgement to Hayley and made his way to the kitchen with Mr Beagle following close behind him. His mother was sitting on a stool next to a shiny white kitchen worktop. On top of the worktop was a plate of chocolate cookies.

Art's face lit up as his mother offered him a cookie. He walked over to his mother and took one of the cookies. As he did this, the side of his jacket with Spiky in opened slightly and Mrs Myatt caught a glimpse of the inside of Art's jacket and his bulging pocket.

'Your jacket pocket looks a little full Art, be careful it doesn't tear.'

Art stepped back away from his mother and nibbled the cookie.

'Er…ok mum, I will,' he said, taking another nibble from the cookie.

Mrs Myatt smiled at Art.

'Ok, Art, I need to leave soon,' she said. 'Are you going to the opening event later?'

'Er…yes, I'm going with Amy.'

'Is that ok with you sister,' Mrs Myatt asked.

'Yes, yes of course, I'm going with Amy's mother. We will all probably meet up at some point later anyway,' Hayley said.

Art felt Spiky move in his jacket pocket. He knew he needed to go to his bedroom and quickly. He pulled his jacket together and stepped slightly back from his mother. He still had half of the cookie left in his hand and Mr Beagle was waiting patiently for some of it.

'I think Mr Beagle has got an eye on the remainder of your cookie Art,' Hayley said.

Art looked at Mr Beagle. Sure enough he was sitting obediently, tail wagging, mouth open waiting for Art's cookie.

Art carefully handed Mr Beagle the remainder of his cookie. Mr Beagle sat on the floor near to Art's feet, eating the cookie.

Art felt Spiky move again.

'Er…if it's ok mum, I need to go upstairs,' Art said.

'Yes, that's fine Art. I'll be leaving in about 20 minutes,' Mrs Myatt said.

Art held his jacket and quickly walked from the kitchen into the hallway and up the stairs to his bedroom, hoping Spiky would stay in his pocket. On his bed was a small cardboard box covered in brown paper and secured tightly with string. Before Art could do anything, Spiky started to climb out of his pocket. Art placed his hands near to his body so he could support him. Spiky climbed into Art's hands and Art carefully placed him on the bed next to the parcel. Art removed his jacket and placed it on a chair.

Mr Beagle arrived in Art's bedroom to find Art and Spiky sitting on the bed together. Art picked up the parcel and started to remove the string and paper. As he did this, Spiky grabbed a large piece of the paper in his mouth and walked across the bed away from Art to eat it.

'Spiky, you can't eat that, give it back to me,' Art said.

Spiky reluctantly let Art take the paper from him and walked back across the bed to Art to cause more mischief. Mr Beagle watched as Spiky tried to climb on Art's lap so he could grab something else from the parcel.

Art managed to remove all of the string and paper and put it out of Spiky's reach. He opened the lid to the box and removed the packaging to find a message written on a piece of beige - coloured paper waiting for him. Art picked up the message to read it.

Dear Art

I guess by now you have found the Little Green Dragon and you are wondering where you are supposed to take him? The Little Green Dragon got lost somehow and should be at Dragon Valley. He will be collected from you on Sunday evening around 7pm. If you could be outside in an open field away from people it would be safer. I suppose your task is to keep The Little Green Dragon safe and away from public interest until then. I know this isn't going to be easy for you so I have placed inside this box a very special torch to help you. It's not just any torch it can produce three-dimensional images projected out in front of you and it will open the gateway to Dragon Valley. Press the button on the side and imagine what you want to see or do and well you'll be amazed, I'm sure. By the way, to anyone else it's just a shiny silver torch.

See you soon,

Samuel

Spiky was now sitting in the box on Art's lap trying to work out what mischief to do next. Art tried to move Spiky so he could take the torch out of the box. Spiky thought Art was playing with him so he made little squeaky noises and nudged his hand with his head. This carried on for several minutes before Art's mother shouted to him from downstairs.

'I'm nearly ready to leave Art, are you coming down to see me off?' she shouted.

Art moved Spiky from his lap, closed the lid to the box and got up from the bed.

'I won't be long Spiky,' said Art, hoping Spiky would behave.

Art checked the bedroom window to ensure it was

shut before walking to the door. Mr Beagle followed Art and exited the room before him. Art closed the door behind him and walked downstairs hoping Spiky wouldn't cause any damage.

CHAPTER NINE

THREE DIMENSIONAL

When Art arrived downstairs his mother had her car keys in her hand waiting to leave. She asked Art not to get in any mischief but to enjoy the fun weekend. Art agreed and asked his mother to drive safely.

Before she left she told Hayley she would check the newspapers at her house about sightings of bright lights at night in the sky above Oxfordshire and sudden disappearances of certain breeds of animals.

Art listened to his mother. He was completely unaware of the newspaper reports. After Mrs Myatt left, Art and Mr Beagle went back upstairs to Art's bedroom leaving Hayley downstairs watching television. When he opened the door, he found Spiky balancing on top of his wardrobe. Art quickly scanned the rest of his room for damage but everything seemed ok. He closed the door behind him, walked over to his bed and removed the torch from the box. He looked at it, turning it at the same time in his hand. It wasn't very big and fitted in Art's hand perfectly.

Art knew Amy was calling for him soon but he wanted to see what the torch actually did. Art held his arm out towards the door and pressed the button on the side of the torch with his thumb. To his amazement a hologram of a three-dimensional image of what he believed to be Dragon Valley projected out in front of him. Art stared at the image. He felt as if he was really standing in Dragon Valley watching as Dragons of all different colours and size flew happily high in the air interacting with each other. Spiky, still sitting on top of the wardrobe, wobbled a bit, made a sharp squeaking noise then flapped his wings and flew directly at the image to join in with the other Dragons. Mr Beagle stayed very close to Art's legs, protecting his tail. Spiky, unaware the image was just a hologram, flew straight through it and crashed into the bedroom door. Art pressed the button on the torch again to stop the hologram. He then rushed over to Spiky to help him. Mr Beagle stayed in the same place, deciding not to move. Art placed the torch in his pocket and lifted Spiky up placing him on the bed. Only Spiky's pride was hurt and he soon flapped his wings to fly back to sit on top of the wardrobe.

Before Art could play with the torch again, Amy arrived downstairs. Art left Spiky sitting up on the wardrobe and went downstairs with Mr Beagle to see her.

'Are you ready Art, it's getting quite busy in the village,' Amy said.

'Er…yes, just need to go and get my jacket. Won't be long,' Art said.

'Art, before you go, what was in the box you received?' Hayley asked.

'Oh, this Aunt Hayley,' said Art, pulling the torch from his pocket. 'It was sent to me by a friend, er…Samuel.'

Art held the torch in his hand out in front of him for Hayley to see.

'Samuel,' said Amy.

'Oh that's nice of him Art,' said Hayley, leaning forwards to look at it. 'Looks like a nice shiny torch. Might be useful later when it gets dark?'

'Er…yes, that's what I thought,' Aunt Hayley, said Art, putting the torch back into his pocket.

'I'll just go upstairs and get my jacket,' Art said.

Art left Amy and Hayley downstairs talking about Brillion's fun weekend. Mr Beagle decided to wait at the bottom of the stairs for Art.

When Art arrived back in his bedroom, Spiky was sitting on his bed. Art put the message from Samuel in his trouser pocket along with the torch before putting his jacket on. Spiky continued to sit on the bed watching Art get ready to leave. Art looked at Spiky and decided it would be better to carry him in his small sports backpack. Art normally used this backpack for sports events to carry small water bottles in. It was expensive and of very good design. Art made sure the backpack was empty before lifting Spiky up and placing him inside. Art left the top slightly open for Spiky to look out. He sat in the backpack quite happily waiting to go on an adventure with Art.

CHAPTER TEN

BRILLIONS OPENING EVENT

Art took one final look at Spikey in his backpack before making his way downstairs. As Art walked, Spiky peeked out of the top of the backpack, looking at the surroundings and Mr Beagle. When he arrived downstairs Hayley was busy in the kitchen and Amy was standing in the hallway tapping her foot and looking impatient.

'Come on Art, we need to go,' Amy said.

'I'm sorry, I needed to get ready,' said Art, holding the backpack out in front of him for Amy to see.

Spiky lifted his head out of the top and puffed some smoke at Amy.

'Oh, I see,' said Amy coughing.

Art handed the backpack to Amy and walked into the kitchen to talk to Hayley. While Art was gone Spiky took the opportunity to look out of the top of the backpack to scan the surroundings. When Art returned, Spiky was still visible and Amy was ready to hand him back the backpack and go to Brillion's opening event.

As they walked down the cottage path, Spiky kept lifting his head out of the backpack. Art tried to gently push him back inside but Spiky thought Art was playing and gently chewed the top of his fingers. Gradually Spiky got tired and fell asleep inside the backpack. Art was relieved and started to tell Amy about the message from Samuel and all about the torch.

Amy listened carefully trying to take in all the information.

'Can't wait to see the torch work Art, it sounds amazing,' Amy said excitedly.

'Yes, I've only seen three-dimensional images like that at Oxford's cinema,' Art said.

They continued walking past the cottages until they reached a place in the village where Amy said she knew a short cut to the sports field. She encouraged Art to take the short cut with her, to avoid getting caught up with other people making their way to the sports field. Art thought only for a moment and agreed. Mr Beagle didn't take any encouraging as he happily walked in front them with his head held high and tail wagging from side to side.

Surprisingly, Spiky was still asleep and behaving himself.

As they got closer to the sports field they could hear Mr Popkiss speaking on the loud speaker. Amy chuckled to herself as she listened to his squeaky voice.

'Testing, 123, er…ladies and gentlemen and er…children…wel…come to… Brillion's er…fun weekend...'

'Who's that,' Art asked.

'It's Mr Popkiss,' Amy said laughing. 'He's a really nice man but he sounds ever so funny when he speaks.'

They continued walking until they reached the edge of the sports field. It was approaching 6pm and people were gathered all around the outside of the field waiting for the announcement of the opening of the fun weekend by a special guest from Snap FM radio station. Inside the field, Art could see line markings ready for the sports afternoon in two day's time.

Everyone got excited and cheered when Mr Popkiss announced he was handing over the microphone to the special guest.

Everyone cheered loudly when the very popular, Harvey Elliot, Snap FM's early morning radio presenter, asked everyone to count down with him from ten. The whole crowd counted down together 10, 9, 8, 7, 6, 5, 4, 3, 2, 1, making Spiky stir a little bit.

'I announce the fun weekend open,' said Harvey.

Everyone cheered again and then music from Snap FM radio station played through loudspeakers waking Spiky fully from his sleep.

Art felt his backpack move in his hand. He looked at it to find Spiky trying to climb out through the top. Amy walked closer to Art to help him hide Spiky from people's sight.

'Art, perhaps we should move away and go and stand over there by the trees,' said Amy, pointing at a group of very tall trees.

'Er-yes, ok,' said Art, following Amy.

They waited by the trees trying to decide what they

could do to pacify Spiky. Mr Beagle wondered close to them sniffing the ground as he moved.

'Perhaps he's hungry,' Amy said.

'Mm, could be I suppose,' said Art. 'Shame he ate all of that plant.'

Spiky continued to try and force his body through the top of the backpack.

'Amy, I don't think I can keep him in this for much longer,' said Art, looking worried.

'You can't force him to stay in it Art. You'll have to let him out.' Amy said.

Mr Beagle noticed Art was having difficulty with Spiky and came running over to him–but not too close.

Spiky looked at Art and made a loud squeaking noise at him before pushing his head upwards. With Art's help he crawled out of the backpack, up his arm and onto Art's shoulder. He sat on Art's shoulder moving his head from side to side looking at all of the people.

Amy looked at Art as he stood motionless with Spiky on his shoulder.

'Well, this is a first Art, you have a Dragon sitting on your shoulder,' Amy said laughing.

'It's not funny Amy,' mumbled Art, looking worried.

Mr Beagle looked on cautiously, hoping Spiky would stay with Art.

Spiky had other ideas. He wanted to explore Brillion and find something to eat. He jumped from Art's shoulder onto the tree and crawled up until he reached a branch he could sit on. He sat nibbling leaves as he looked out across the sports field and to where Mr Popkiss was helping out with cooking sausages on a barbeque. He sat on the branch for a few more moments before making a hungry, squeaking noise and flying off across the sports field to get his dinner.

'What do we do now?' Art said.

'There's nothing we can do Art. Perhaps we should wait here for a few moments to see if he returns,' Amy said.

Mr Beagle barked gently in agreement.

Spiky hovered high in the air waiting for the moment he could dive and get his dinner.

Luckily for him, people thought he was just another bird hovering in the sky.

Below, the Stacey triplets: Billy, Jack and Simon were waiting at the barbeque for their hotdogs. As they waited, they teased Mr Popkiss.

'Hurry up Mr Popkiss, I'm starving,' Billy said laughing.

'Er...123...123, hotdog please...123...123,' said Jack, also laughing.

Mr Popkiss gave them their hotdogs and they moved away from the barbeque to go and sit at a table away from the crowd. They were greedy and each triplet ordered two hotdogs and two spare sausages each with tomato sauce.

'I need a drink,' Billy said.

'So do I,' Jack said.

'Me too,' Simon said.

Spiky watched as Simon laid his spare hotdogs on a napkin on the table and went to the drinks stall to order cold drinks for himself and his brothers. While he was gone Jack and Billy munched away at their hotdogs, completely unaware Spiky was hovering high in the air above them. The brothers continued eating their food before getting impatient waiting for their drinks to arrive. They both looked at Simon and shouted at him to hurry up.

Spiky immediately dived straight down to the table just like a lightning bolt, grabbing Simon's two sausages with his claws. As he lifted the sausages up the napkin also flew up in the air landing on Billy's face, covering him with tomato sauce.

'What's going on,' said Billy, trying to remove the napkin.

Jack pointed and laughed at his brother's misfortune.

Simon heard all the noise and returned back quickly with the cold drinks.

He looked at Billy with tomato sauce on his face and accused him of eating his spare sausages. Billy dismissed his brother's accusations and told him it must have been a bird who stole his sausages. To keep the peace Billy offered to buy him two more.

Spiky however, was far away from the triplets, sitting back in the tree where Art and Amy were standing.

Art and Amy watched as Spiky sat on a branch above them tucking into the sausages.

'Well, at least we know he's not a vegetarian,' Amy said.

'Yes, but I wonder who he took them from?' Art said.

Art and Amy waited for Spiky to finish eating and to their surprise he crawled back down the tree to sit on Art's shoulder again. Art opened his backpack hoping Spiky would get back inside. Spiky was having none of it. He wanted to explore more of Brillion. He hopped back onto the tree, crawled back up to the branch, flapped his wings and flew high up in the air, disappearing into the distant clouds.

Art and Amy decided they could do nothing at the moment to get Spiky back and that he would hopefully find them if he wanted to. Amy noticed Hayley and her mother on the far side of the sports field. They walked quickly to go and see them before following event signs leading them into the village centre. They collected some advertising brochures for the fun weekend and made their way back to outside Amy's cottage.

By now it was getting late and both Hayley and Amy's mother had already returned to their own cottages.

Art and Amy talked for a few minutes before agreeing to meet outside the front of the cottages at 10:00 am the next day.

CHAPTER ELEVEN

SLADES CREW

The next morning when Art first woke up, he looked out of his bedroom window for some sign of Spiky. In his heart he was hoping Spiky would have found his way back and would be sitting on the windowsill, but when he looked there was no sign of him. Art knew he needed to find Spiky before Sunday and hoped that he would return very soon.

While Art continued to look out of his window Hayley called him down to eat his breakfast. When Art arrived downstairs he noticed that Mr Beagle was missing. Hayley told Art she let him out in the garden earlier and he hadn't returned back yet.

Art guessed Mr Beagle had gone exploring, but he promised Hayley he would go and look for Mr Beagle after he finished his breakfast and before going to see Amy.

This pleased Hayley very much.

During breakfast, which Art was enjoying, he asked his Aunt Hayley if she had spoken to his mother. Hayley told him his mother got back home safely and would be calling her later that day. He also asked her about the missing dogs and the sudden disappearances of certain breeds of animals his mother mentioned. Hayley told Art she would probably know more when his mother called her.

Art finished his breakfast and went into the back garden for a walk and to find Mr Beagle. As Art walked down the lawn he scanned one side of the garden, then the other side of the garden searching for any sign or movement of Mr Beagle. This continued right down to the bottom of the garden where Art stopped, watched and listened to four men talking loudly to each other standing on a grass area just outside the forest.

'It was last seen flying high over there into the trees,' said the first man loudly.

'Let's go and see if we can find it. Probably get lots of money for it, if we can capture it and take it back to Mill Lane,' said the second man.

'Yeh, I agree,' said the third man. 'I've brought nets and sacks with me so it can't escape.'

'And I've brought food to tempt it down from the trees,' said the fourth man holding up a string of sausages in the air.

Art wondered if it was Spiky they were talking about. He stood very still and quiet continuing to look and listen to the men. He didn't recognize any of them and they wore black coloured t-shirts with a white logo printed on the back saying Slade's Crew. The men continued talking to each other before disappearing one by one into the forest.

Art waited patiently and listened. But as the men walked deeper into the forest their voices became fainter and fainter. Eventually everything fell deadly silent. For a time not even the birds made a sound.

Art stayed at the bottom of the garden hoping Mr Beagle or even Spiky would soon appear. He listened, then suddenly it was as if the forest exploded. First he heard a loud bang! Then scuffles from inside the forest; then he saw birds flying from the trees high up into the sky trying to escape. But he wasn't sure what they were trying to escape from.

Another loud bang echoed from inside the forest making Art jump. This was followed by the sound of Mr Beagle barking very loudly. Next he heard members of Slade's Crew cheering as they made more noise disturbing the occupants of the whole forest.

Art next heard Mr Beagle howl loudly, then out through the tops of the trees flew Spiky. He looked bigger and stronger as he flew up into the air and glided beautifully in the sky, stopping to hover just above the forest.

The men from Slade's Crew ran from the forest out into an open area. They looked up at Spiky shouting at him as they waved their nets and sausages in the air. Spiky continued to hover above the forest looking down into the trees, ignoring Slade's Crew for the moment.

A few seconds later, Mr Beagle appeared from a gap in the forest not very far away from Slade's Crew.

To get back home quickly he needed to run past Slade's Crew.

This didn't bother Mr Beagle so he raised his head

and started to run slowly through the long grass. As he approached Slade's Crew one of the men shouted at Mr Beagle, blaming him for Spiky's escape. In anger and without thinking, the man threw one of his nets at Mr Beagle. The net spun around and around in the air gathering speed as it headed straight for Mr Beagle. Spiky still watching from above, saw the net and before it could reach Mr Beagle he swooped down extremely fast and caught it in his claws. Mr Beagle continued running, making a slight barking noise of acknowledgement to Spiky as he continued past Slade's Crew and back to Art.

Spiky flew back up in the air and stopped immediately over the man who threw the net at Mr Beagle. Before the man could move, Spiky dropped the net on his head before flying back up into the sky away from Slade's Crew. The man tried to free himself but the more he moved, the more tangled in his net he got. His friends laughed at him as he tried time and time again to free himself.

'Serves you right,' said one of the other men helping him. 'You said no-one could escape your nets.'

'I'll get that bird or whatever it is sooner or later,' said the man, finally managing to untangle himself.

Spiky swooped down towards Slade's Crew several times deliberately annoying them before flying up into the sky disappearing into the clouds and out of sight.

Eventually Slade's Crew gave up on catching Spiky. They gathered their belongings and left the forest to walk back to Brillion.

Art waited for Slade's Crew to leave before walking back up the lawn to the cottage with Mr Beagle.

CHAPTER TWELVE

IMPORTANT ANNOUNCEMENT

Once inside the cottage Art explained to Hayley that he had found Mr Beagle just outside the forest. Hayley was happy with his explanation and made a fuss of Mr Beagle. While Art went upstairs to his bedroom to get ready Hayley took the opportunity to give Mr Beagle some food and water. This pleased Mr Beagle as he was hungry and thirsty after the early events of the morning.

When Art arrived downstairs he found Hayley standing near Mr Beagle watching him finishing his food.

'Mr Beagle is a very gentle dog Art isn't he?' Hayley said.

Art looked at Mr Beagle and smiled before replying.

'Yes, he is Aunt Hayley,' Art said. 'I think he is very special.'

Mr Beagle lifted his ears up slightly to listen to the

compliments while he finished the remainder of his food.

Art looked at him again noticing he was listening.

'Are you ready to leave Mr Beagle?' Art asked.

Mr Beagle looked up at Art and wagged his tail fast. He then turned and walked towards the front door and sat upright waiting patiently for Art.

'It looks like Mr Beagle is waiting for you Art,' said Hayley, smiling.

'Yes, thank you Aunt Hayley. Are you doing anything today?' Art asked.

'I'm popping down to my shop this morning and meeting up with some of my friends this afternoon Art,' Hayley said. 'But I'll be here at lunchtime, so don't forget to come back to the cottage at 1pm for some lunch Art.'

'Ok, Aunt Hayley, that's sounds great,' said Art, rubbing his stomach. 'See you later.'

Art checked his pocket for the Traveller's Map and torch before walking to the front door and opening it.

Hayley watched as Mr Beagle raised his tail and bounced confidently out through the open doorway onto the steps outside. Art walked outside and closed the door behind him. As he did so, Amy called to him.

'Hurry up Art. How long do I have to wait for you to get ready?' she said, teasing him.

Art pretended to ignore Amy and started to walk down the path towards the gate. On hearing Amy's voice, Mr Beagle left Art behind as he ran in front of him making his way to where Amy was standing.

As Art got closer to Amy she teased him a little bit more.

'Did you over-sleep Art?'

'Er-no there was a kind of disturbance involving Spiky in the forest this morning and I had to go and find Mr Beagle,' Art said.

'Oh, I see, but what kind of disturbance?'

'Er…it involved some people called Slade's Crew. I think they were trying to catch Spiky but he was too clever for them,' Art said. 'He looked a bit bigger and he was fast, really fast. I really don't know how I am going to keep him safe and away from people until Sunday.'

'My mum mentioned something about Slade's Crew to me before I left. Trouble is I can't remember what she told me. Anyhow, I'm sure you'll think of something Art. Come on let's go and see what's happening in the village,' she said, grabbing his arm to encourage him to walk with her.

Art didn't need much encouragement. He walked happily with Amy along the front of the cottages chatting casually about school. Mr Beagle raised his tail and bounced along the path in front of them.

When they arrived in the village it was really busy with people visiting Brillion and wanting to join in with the fun weekend. Music played from loud speakers and many different activities were taking place throughout the village. As they walked, the music from the loud speakers stopped and Mr Popkiss started to speak. Art and Amy stopped and listened to what he had to say.

'Er…ladies and gentlemen and er…children wel…come to… Brillion's…fun weekend…I…have an important…announ…cement to…make. Due to…unfore…seen cir…cumstances the…trea…sure hunt has been…cancelled. We…hope you en…joy

67

yourself…and join…in with the other fun and activities. Er…thank you'

Mr Popkiss stopped speaking and music resumed through the loud speakers.

'What was all that about?' Amy said.

'Don't know,' said Art, chuckling to himself.

Just at that same moment they heard a man and woman standing near them talking to each other.

'They cancelled the treasure hunt down to Mill Lane because someone's stolen the prizes, of all things,' said the woman shaking her head.

'Really, must be some petty thieves,' said the man.

'My friend also told me the parish council is considering cancelling the walk to Ghost Camp in the forest because of a report of a large flying bird. Apparently, someone from the parish council has paid for a team of animal catchers calling themselves Slade's Crew, to catch the bird. Whatever next!' said the woman. 'It's probably just a Red Kite.'

'Let's hope they sort it all out soon,' said the man.

Art and Amy continued walking, moving away from the couple.

'Sounds like they were talking about Spiky' Amy said.

'Yes, I know but it's a shame they had to stop the treasure hunt. Where is Mill Lane Amy?'

'It's off one of the roads leading into the village. No one ever goes down Mill Lane. There's an old farmhouse. The lane's overgrown with hedges and things and it's dark and scary.' Amy said.

'Mm, just the place to be hiding something,' Art said.

'Art, No…I'm not going down that lane.'

'Oh come on Amy I've just got a hunch. What could possibly go wrong? You want to go, don't you Mr Beagle?' said Art smiling.

Mr Beagle looked up at Art and wagged his tail fast around and around just like a propeller.

'See, Mr Beagle wants to go Amy.'

 Amy was silent for a moment.

'Ok, I'll take you Art, but we must be back for 1pm and don't forget we are supposed to be going to Marlock's opening event this afternoon.'

'That's fine with me Amy, I told my Aunt Hayley I would be back for 1pm,' Art said.

Amy led the way as all three of them made their way from the village centre to Mill Lane.

CHAPTER THIRTEEN

THE LITTLE BIT OF CRIME

It took them 15 minutes to walk to Mill Lane and when they arrived they found the entrance to the lane completely blocked by thick tree branches covered with leaves. Mr Beagle walked over to the entrance and started to sniff the ground searching for a way in. After a few moments he let out a low growl as he continued to move around the front of the entrance. By this time Art and Amy had walked closer to the entrance.

'See Art, there's no way in,' said Amy, pointing at the tree branches.

'There must be some way in Amy,' said Art, scanning the entrance and surrounding area.

'Come on Art, let's go back to the village,' Amy said.

'In a minute Amy, I just want to look.' He noticed the surrounding area was protected by a tall thick hedgerow with a wire fence in front of it.

Art suddenly remembered the torch Samuel sent him and wondered if it could show them anything beyond the blocked entrance. He searched his pockets for it and removed it.

'Amy wait!' said Art, holding the torch up in the air. 'I've brought the torch, it might show us something.'

Amy looked at him with a puzzled look on her face.

Art held the torch in his right hand and pointed it at the entrance. He then pressed the button on the side and a three-dimensional image of a road appeared in front of them replacing the tree branches. Art moved the torch and the image moved up along the road towards a building.

'Wow!' Amy said.

Mr Beagle, who was standing just in front of Art, walked closer to the image. He sat upright staring at it as Art moved the torch a little bit further to show the building and a yard with a little red tractor with big, shiny head lights and long metal forks attached to it.

'Art, that's amazing,' Amy said.

Mr Beagle barked in agreement.

'Yes, and I think we now know how the entrance was blocked,' said Art, now moving the torch away from the tractor to show the inside of the building.

Inside the building lying on the floor were nets, sacks and different kinds of big torches. Art moved the torch a little bit more and they could see Slade's Crew standing next to three long wooden tables.

Art focused on the tables.

'Art look,' said Amy, pointing at the image. 'It looks like they've been stealing.'

Lying carefully on top of the tables were personal

items belonging to people – wallets, purses, watches, cameras, money and Brillion's treasure hunt prizes.

Art moved the torch again to show metal objects standing on the floor at the back of the room. As the image became clearer they could see large metal cages Slade's Crew used for keeping animals inside.

Mr Beagle immediately growled loudly in disapproval and moved closer to the image, almost touching his nose on it. Then without any warning, he leapt at the image and before Art could do anything he crashed into the tree branches and yelped out loud in discomfort.

Art quickly pressed the torch again to stop the image and walked to Mr Beagle to help him. With Amy's help he got Mr Beagle untangled and checked he wasn't hurt.

Mr Beagle enjoyed the fuss and decided to sit on the ground in front of the tree branches and rest. As Art and Amy were deciding what to do next they both heard the tractor's engine start up and a man speaking loudly to the tractor driver.

'Go and clear the entrance for us, we need to go back to the forest to try and capture that bird for Popkiss,' the man said.

'Will do,' said the tractor driver, starting up the tractor.

Next, Art and Amy could hear the sound of the tractor driving down from the building towards the entrance.

Mr Beagle got up from the ground and growled.

'Art, we need to go,' Amy said. 'I know a different way back across the fields, follow me quickly.'

'Er…yes, ok,' said Art, listening to Mr Beagle

growling. 'Come on Mr Beagle - follow us,' he said, trying to encourage Mr Beagle to follow him.

Mr Beagle gave a final growl of disapproval and walked to join Art to follow Amy back to the village.

*

When Art, Amy and Mr Beagle arrived back at the village it was very busy with people enjoying fun activities. It was also getting close to 12:30 and nearly time for lunch. As they were getting ready to go back to the cottages, Amy noticed that people were gathering in one particular place in the street. It was next to a Maypole and they were laughing and cheering at something or someone?

'I've got to see what all the fuss is about,' Amy said.

Amy, Art and Mr Beagle walked over to where the people were standing enjoying themselves. They squeezed themselves carefully through the crowd only to find the Maypole decorated with pink and white ribbons and with people dancing around it.

'Amy…is that the Stacey Triplets dancing around the Maypole?' asked Art, trying not to laugh.

'Oh, yes and it looks like Mr Popkiss is joining in with them too,' said Amy, laughing.

'What do they look like!' Art said.

Mr Beagle barked in agreement.

'Come on Art let's go before I split my sides laughing,' said Amy, wiping away tears of laughter from her eyes.

They squeezed themselves back out through the crowd and started to make their way to Amy's cottage. When they arrived, they were still laughing at what they had just witnessed and for a moment they forgot all about Mill Lane and Slade's Crew.

'I'll meet you out here at 2pm Art, it will give us enough time to get to our seats at Marlock's marquee' said Amy, walking down the path to her cottage. 'Can't wait to see what's going to happen!'

'Ok, see you then,' Art said. 'Come on Mr Beagle, lunch time.'

CHAPTER FOURTEEN

MARLOCKS MARQUEE OF WONDERS

Art arrived inside his Aunt Hayley's cottage to discover she had already prepared him some lunch and filled Mr Beagle's dishes with food and water.

Art chatted with his Aunt Hayley while he ate his lunch. They discussed the activities in the village and Art told his Aunt Hayley about the Maypole dancing. After lunch Art decided to go up to his bedroom to rest before going to the marquee with Amy. Mr Beagle followed Art to his bedroom and decided to rest on the carpet next to his bed.

Art checked his pockets for the Traveller's Map and Torch before walking over to the window. He opened it wide hoping to see Spiky sitting outside in the trees.

He didn't have to wait very long because Spiky was waiting for him.

As soon as he saw Art looking through the window

he flew from the nearby trees, spreading his wings fully, diving downwards then back upwards before finally settling on the window-ledge balancing half in and half out of the window. He steadied himself and lent forwards inside the window. Art looked at Spiky. He was stronger and getting bigger.

Art tried to encourage Spiky further inside, but Spiky had other ideas and wanted to stay outside where he was free to fly and to watch the Brillion activities from high in the sky. He could also grab some sausages when he wanted to.

In the meantime, Mr Beagle moved closer to the bedroom door hiding his tail. He sat upright watching and waiting to see what Spiky would do next.

Spiky made friendly squeaking noises to Art before letting out a puff of smoke from his nose. Art walked forwards, closer towards him and Spiky let out another puff of smoke from his nose before slowly turning himself around on the window ledge and flying back towards the trees.

Art smiled at Spiky as he watched him showing off his flying skills by bobbing up and down between the branches, brushing his wings against the leaves before landing at speed on a branch at the top of one of the trees. Art waved to Spiky before closing his bedroom window.

He was conscious of the time and didn't want to be late to meet Amy. Art quickly checked his room and walked downstairs. After speaking to his Aunt Hayley he went outside with Mr Beagle to meet Amy.

Amy was waiting for him and as they walked to the marquee, Art told her about the visit from Spiky. She listened carefully to Art as they walked past people laughing and joking as they enjoyed themselves at the fun weekend. They soon arrived at the marquee to find Marlock standing outside greeting people. Sitting obediently next to him was Star.

'Welcome Art and Amy to my very special opening event,' Marlock said. 'Please go inside and take your seats. I'll be with you soon…'

Mr Beagle walked over to Star and stayed with him for a few moments before going inside the marquee with Art and Amy. He followed them to their seats at the front row of the marquee. They sat down next to each other with Mr Beagle lying on the floor just in front of them.

Art looked around him at the inside of the marquee. Deep blue coloured cloth, decorated with golden zigzag patterns, hung downwards from the roof. It was secured to the sides of the marquee with blue and white coloured rope. Sparkling white lights bolted to the floor shone up onto the cloth, bouncing off the patterns and creating a dazzling display of golden shapes in the marquee high above them.

People started to join them inside the marquee and the loud noise of people talking to each other soon echoed throughout the marquee. Slowly the seats were full and everyone waited eagerly for the show to start. Mr Beagle nodded, placing his head on the ground, catching a quick sleep while he could. Section by section the audience went very quiet waiting, wondering what would happen first.

Music sounded from speakers fitted to the inside of the marquee and different coloured lights shone across the stage. Without notice, Marlock and a group of male and female dancers ran onto the stage. The dancers moved effortlessly across the stage dancing while Marlock walked to the front of the stage, bowing to the audience as they clapped and cheered.

Art and Amy joined the other people clapping as they watched the dancers perform. Mr Beagle now fast asleep slept through the whole introduction.

When the dancers stopped, Marlock introduced himself to everyone as a magician and started to perform different magical acts, making the audience cheer and clap even louder.

Art and Amy were enjoying themselves very much joining in with the rest of the audience watching as Marlock performed his magical tricks using fantastic coloured lighting, imaginary smoke and many different props.

Time passed quickly as Marlock continued to perform magical tricks one after another impressing Art, Amy and everyone in the audience.

Mr Beagle stayed fast asleep.

This continued for over an hour until it came to the finale. Marlock stopped performing magic and stood at the front of the stage looking at the audience moving his eyes from one side then to the other side until he stopped and looked directly at Art.

'I need a volunteer,' Marlock said.

'Here, here, pick me,' people shouted from the audience holding their hands up into the air.

Marlock paused as he pretended to look at the people with their hands up. He moved his eyes across the audience before stopping to look at Art again.

'I think I may have found a volunteer,' Marlock said. 'Please give a big round of applause for Art Myatt.'

The audience clapped and cheered very loudly encouraging Art to join Marlock.

Art turned to look at Amy.

'Come on Art,' Marlock said. 'You'll be quite safe.'

The audience continued shouting and cheering.

'I don't think you've got much choice Art,' said Amy, feeling worried.

Mr Beagle woke from his deep sleep and sat up to look at Art.

Art got up from his seat and started to walk slowly to the stage steps. He climbed them one by one wondering what cunning plan Marlock had in mind for him. When he reached the stage, Marlock grabbed his arm and walked him to the centre of the stage making the audience cheer and stamp their feet in excitement.

Amy and Mr Beagle watched as Marlock looked directly at the middle of the audience before raising his arms straight up in the air. Seconds passed and without notice, all of the lights in the marquee went out.

The audience murmured before going deadly silent.

Amy sat in her seat with Mr Beagle sitting close to her feet wondering what was going on. She looked but could only see darkness.

'That wasn't supposed to happen,' Marlock said.

'Don't worry,' said Art, without thinking. 'I've got a torch in my pocket.'

Art moved his hand to the inside of his pocket and grabbed the torch. He removed it and pressed the button on the side and held it out in front of him. The whole of the marquee in front of him lit up with a beautiful, soft, calming white light.

Art could see all of the audience and Amy with Mr Beagle.

'Don't panic everyone. Normal service will resume very soon,' said Marlock, looking for his assistants.

Art continued to hold the torch out in front of him while Marlock disappeared from stage. Art could hear people speaking and loud clanging noises from the side of the marquee. Suddenly, section by section, the marquee lit back up and Art pressed the button on the torch to turn it off.

Marlock appeared back on stage and stood in the middle to talk to the audience.

'I apologize for any inconvenience ladies and gentlemen. I hope you enjoyed the other parts of the show. Thank you to Art Myatt for bringing er…such a bright torch with him,' said Marlock looking for Art.

Art had already walked away from Marlock down the steps and off the stage to join Amy and Mr Beagle. The other people in the audience got up from their seats and started to leave through exits situated around the marquee. Art, Amy and Mr Beagle followed them outside.

As they started to walk away from the marquee, Marlock was walking fast to catch up with them.

'Art wait, how did you get that torch?' Marlock asked.

Art didn't want to tell him Samuel sent it to him, so he pretended he didn't hear Marlock and continued walking away from the marquee with Amy and Mr Beagle.

'It must have been Samuel,' shouted Marlock, deciding to stop walking. 'Look after it Art, you will need it if you hope to open the gateway to Dragon Valley!'

CHAPTER FIFTEEN

MR BEAGLE TO THE RESCUE

'Did you hear what he shouted Art?' Amy said.

'Er…yes, something about Dragon Valley,' Art said.

'Well, what is it?' Amy asked.

'Don't really know,' Art said. 'Samuel mentioned something about it in his letter to me. I'll look at it again when I go back to the cottage later. Come on let's go and look around the village centre.'

Most of the roads had been closed so it was easy for people to walk safely around the village and enjoy the activities without the worry of moving vehicles.

Mr Beagle led the way and with his tail upright, he walked proudly in front of Art and Amy. When they arrived people were dancing around the Maypole enjoying themselves and volunteers from the village were running various fun games to entertain the visitors.

'This is really cool Art, I didn't know Brillion could be so much fun,' Amy said.

'Er…yes, Amy,' said Art, walking slowly looking at the activities.

As they continued walking, Amy spotted a group of table-top stalls where people were selling bric-a-brac items. She wanted to go and look so she quickly ran across to the stalls leaving Art with Mr Beagle. As Art waited, he noticed an area just a short distance away with a small gathering of amusements.

'Mm…perhaps we should go and look at the amusements while we're waiting for Amy,' said Art, looking at Mr Beagle.

Mr Beagle didn't need much convincing. He was happy to follow Art anywhere.

Before he moved, Art looked across at Amy at the bric-a-brac stalls. He was trying to catch her attention so he could let her know where he was going. He smiled to himself as he could see her searching through the items on the tables.

'Looks like Amy's busy Mr Beagle, let's go, I'm sure she'll find us' Art said.

He was about to walk to the amusements when he heard someone nearby shouting for help.

'My purse, I've lost my purse,' shouted a distressed woman nearby. 'Please help me find it.'

Art looked across at the woman. She was with her husband standing next to an ice cream van. Her face looked panic stricken. People started to gather around her helping to look for her purse.

Mr Beagle growled in disapproval and walked quickly over to where the woman was standing. He first went close to the woman, weaving between people legs, sniffing the ground. Next, he moved away sniffing the ground again as he walked, following the tracks of where the woman had been.

By this time, Amy had returned back to where Art was standing. They both looked on with admiration as Mr Beagle tried to find the woman's purse.

'I haven't seen Slade's Crew here,' Art said.

'I hope it's just fallen out of her pocket Art,' said Amy, walking to follow Mr Beagle.

Art joined Amy and only just a short distance away from where the woman was standing, Mr Beagle stopped next to a clump of overgrown rough grass. He moved something with his nose then raised his head and let out a loud howl making people look at him.

Art and Amy rushed over to where he was standing and looked down to the ground to see a red coloured purse.

'You've found it Mr Beagle. Well done!' Said Amy, ruffling his ears.

'Excellent job Mr Beagle, you're a star!' Art said.

The woman rushed over with her husband to where Mr Beagle was standing. She bent down and picked up the purse.

'Oh thank you. Look this clever dog has found my purse' said the woman to her husband.

Mr Beagle sat next to Art taking in compliments.

Other people helping to look for the purse gathered around.

'What's his name,' asked the woman looking at Art.

'His name is Mr Beagle,' said Art proudly.

Chapter Sixteen

A STARTLING APPEARANCE

On the way back to the cottages, Mr Beagle walked confidently in front of Art and Amy as they chatted to each other about his marvelous achievement.

Amy told Art she was going with her parents to Oxford at 6 pm and it was unlikely she would be back early so they arranged to meet outside the front of the cottages at 09:15 am the next day. Amy reminded Art about the sports day and she told him she hoped he was still going to enter some of the sports competitions.

*

Later that evening, Art sat on his bed and Mr Beagle was lying on the floor stretched fully out under his bedroom window fast asleep.

Hayley was very pleased to hear the story of Mr Beagle finding the missing purse. She made a big fuss of Mr Beagle before leaving him alone in the cottage with Art for the evening while she went into the village with a friend.

This gave Art time to re-cap on the day's events and to start thinking about the big sports day. While he was re-capping he looked out of his bedroom window several times for some sighting of Spiky - but there was no sign of him.

As the evening progressed darkness crept slowly into the bedroom, engulfing Art and Mr Beagle. Hayley was still in the village with her friend so instead of switching the bedroom light on, Art decided to use the torch hoping it would work just like it did at Marlock's marquee.

He held the torch out in front of him towards the bedroom window and pressed the button on the side. To his amazement, instead of beautiful, soft, calming white light, a real-time virtual image of Samuel appeared in front of him standing in Dragon Valley.

Art sat up on his bed still holding the torch in front of him, slightly startled. He could also see Dragons of all different sizes flying in the sky behind Samuel.

Mr Beagle woke from his sleep and barked gently to greet Samuel, then he moved quickly towards the bedroom door to get away from the Dragons.

'Sorry about the sudden appearance Art. Hello Mr Beagle,' said Samuel, smiling at him.

'I've got to be quick Art. Things have changed slightly. You need to go to'…Samuel's image flickered…'tomorrow to the open area just outside the forest called Oak Meadow and use the torch to open the gateway to Dragon Valley. Spiky will follow you,'…Samuel's image flickered again.

'What time Samuel?' said Art, feeling worried.

Art watched as Samuel's image slowly re-appeared in front of him. Dragons seemed to fly close behind Samuel, nearly hitting him with their wings.

'At 7 pm…don't be late or the Dragons may try and find another way to come to Brillion and that would be a disaster,' said Samuel, slowly disappearing in front of Art.

The image of Dragon Valley stayed out in front of Art for a few moments longer. He could still see Dragons flying in the valley. He continued staring at the image, hoping to see Samuel again but instead, without warning, the face of a very large, angry looking green and yellow Dragon appeared in front of him with smoke coming out of its nose.

Art panicked and quickly pressed the button on the torch. The image disappeared instantly leaving him shaken. He put the torch inside his pocket and switched the light on in his bedroom. As he was drawing his bedroom curtains, he heard Hayley opening the front door to the cottage. On hearing Hayley, Art and Mr Beagle left the bedroom to go and see her.

Hayley greeted Mr Beagle warmly by fussing him and giving him a small piece of chocolate biscuit. She then spoke to Art.

'Art you look like you've seen a ghost or something. Are you alright?'

'Yes, I'm fine Aunt Hayley,' Art said. 'I'm just tired.'

'Ok, perhaps an early night will do you good Art. After all it's sports day tomorrow and I've been telling my friends about you and how I think you'll do well,' she said proudly.

'Er…yes, I hope so,' said Art, still thinking about

the image he had just seen.

Shortly afterwards Art went to bed to try and get a good night's sleep, leaving Mr Beagle downstairs with Hayley.

Chapter Seventeen

A Good Idea

Art woke up very early the next morning to the aroma of Hayley baking downstairs. Everywhere he moved upstairs in the cottage, he smelt freshly baked cakes and bread, making him feel very relaxed and hungry.

Before he came down for breakfast he changed into his sports outfit and wore his blue coloured rugby tracksuit on top. The memory of the fierce - looking Dragon, still haunted him slightly but he was trying to focus on sports day. He placed his clothes and shoes in his sports bag along with the torch and Traveller's Map and made his way to the kitchen. When he arrived in the kitchen, Mr Beagle was sitting on the floor observing Hayley, also hoping to get a treat.

While Art sat eating his breakfast, Hayley updated him on her telephone conversations with his mother. She also told him his mother wished him luck at sports day. This pleased Art very much because he missed her when she was not around.

Hayley also told Art that his mother had found the newspaper articles on the sudden disappearances of certain breeds of animals in Oxfordshire and how the Police suspected a local gang for the crime. She looked at Mr Beagle while she told Art about how the gang steal certain breeds of animals and hold them for a ransom. She also told Art she had passed on the information to her friend on the parish council and how they are stepping up the search for farmer Calloway's Basset Hound and the missing Shiz-tzu dog, Tibbles.

As Art continued to listen to his Aunt Hayley he started to think about Slade's Crew at Mill Lane and he wondered to himself if they were also involved in stealing animals.

'Aunt Hayley,' Art said, interrupting. 'Has anyone from the council really looked into Slade's Crew? I mean, Amy and I saw them yesterday heading towards Mill Lane and near to the forest acting really suspicious.'

'Mm…I don't know Art. Perhaps I should mention something to my friend on the parish council. I understand Mr Popkiss hired them,' said Hayley, now deep in thought.

'Sounds like a good idea to me Aunt Hayley. Better go and get ready now,' said Art, as he left the kitchen to go upstairs and collect his sports bag.

CHAPTER EIGHTEEN

SPORTS DAY

Sports Day started at 09:45 am and on the way to the sports field, Art explained to Amy all about the unexpected appearance from Samuel and how he needed to be at Oak Meadow later at 7 pm. Mr Beagle walked in front of them with his ears raised listening.

When they arrived at the sports field Art was greeted by members from the sports day organizing committee. They noted Art's name in their register, gave him a blue number 7 badge to pin on his shirt and directed him to go to the sports building at the edge of the field so he could lock away his sports bag and change back into his casual clothes at the end of the day.

Art entered for three field competitions, Shot Put, Discus, Javelin, and the final event of the day: one final track competition (six laps of the running track), at 1:30 pm, where a village cup could be won. He tried to encourage Amy to join in but she told him she preferred to observe instead of competing. She also told him she needed to look after Mr Beagle.

The field was buzzing with children taking part in competitions and parents following them around. A man's voice tried to announce the next competition through loud speakers but he kept getting overshadowed by the Snap FM radio presenter playing different types of music.

Art entered his first competition - Shot Put at mid-day and came first. Next he entered Discus Throwing at 1pm and came second. He was due to enter the Javelin competition at 2 pm but ten minutes before it was due to start, it was cancelled, because of safety reasons.

He still had one hour until his final competition so Art decided to rest on the grass at the side of the sports field with Amy and Mr Beagle. They watched as competitions started and finished and how people seemed to be enjoying themselves at sports day.

Amy started to feel thirsty, so she went to a nearby parked cold drinks van to buy three bottles of water; one for her, one for Art and one to share with Mr Beagle. While she was waiting in the queue, a discussion started in front of her between a man and a woman about three twelve year old boys from Oxford who had been training to run six laps of the running track for six weeks leading up to the sports day and how any one of them was odds on favorite to win the Brillion village cup.

After Amy paid for the bottles of water, she hurried back to Art to tell him about the conversations she heard. Art wasn't too worried because he trained frequently at rugby training and he told Amy he was only entering the race for fun – but it would be nice to win.

The final event of the day approached and Art stood up to get ready. He looked across at the running track where he could see spectators gathering all around the outside of the track. He left Amy and Mr Beagle to make his way to the starting line. When he arrived, just about everybody at sports day had gathered to witness the final event.

Art waited as three older boys wearing matching red t-shirts and two girls roughly the same age, joined him.

Before the race started, a murmur echoed around the track about the three boys and how they had trained so hard.

Art and the other five competitors were asked to get themselves ready. They waited at the starting line, ready to race. A Snap FM radio presenter counted down - ready, steady and go! Art and the others started to run and the spectators shouted and screamed for their favorite runner.

Art decided to conserve his energy by spacing the race out over the six laps, but soon realized after one lap, his plan might not be any good because the three boys had already started their second lap leaving him and the girls behind. Art pushed himself as hard as he could, but it seemed hopeless as the boys pushed further and further ahead. Amy, Hayley and some of Hayley's friends, shouted for Art, encouraging him to keep going. Art did and when lap six approached the boys slowed, desperately trying to keep moving. Art passed the first boy, then the second boy and ran to catch the third boy. The girls followed Art but they were also struggling to keep running and slowed.

Everyone around the track shouted and cheered as Art ran as hard as he could trying to catch up with the final boy and pass him. There was only a short distance to the finishing line and the third boy slowed right down nearly stopping, leaving Art to run past him and win the race. The noise in the sports field was deafening as everyone cheered for Art and to encourage the other runners to finish.

Art felt very tired and sat on the ground to rest. As he did, Amy and Mr Beagle joined him. The other runners crossed the finishing line one by one.

'Well done Art,' Amy said. 'I knew you would win.'

'Er…thanks Amy,' said Art, taking deep breaths.

Mr Beagle sat close to Art, placing his head on his leg as Art stroked his ears.

*

The sports day presentations commenced at 3 pm where everyone who took part was awarded a certificate signed by the leader of the parish council.

A special presentation was then held for the winner of the final event and Art was asked to collect his Brillion Village Cup from a Snap FM radio presenter. Amy watched along with Hayley and everyone else, as Art proudly received it.

The sports event closed shortly afterwards leaving people enough time to get ready for the evening's Midsummer Night's Ball.

Amy and Mr Beagle waited for Art as he walked to the sports building to collect his sports bag and to get changed.

CHAPTER NINETEEN

THE BREAK IN

When Art arrived at the sports building, a distressed looking Mr Popkiss was leaving the building shouting.

'Break…in…someone has broken in…to our sports…club,' Mr Popkiss shouted.

On hearing Mr Popkiss, Art rushed inside the building to find people frantically searching through clothes for their belongings. Everything inside was upside down with sports bags scattered open across the floor.

Art looked for his sports bag trying not to step on people's clothes. While Art searched, two men from the sports day organizing committee, entered the building speaking loudly to each other.

'It must be Slade's Crew,' said the first man.

'Yes, I agree, we must alert the Police,' said the second man.

Art listened to the men but still continued looking

for his sports bag and clothes. With some help from other people inside the building he eventually found his sports bag open and although his clothes were still inside, he knew someone had been searching through his belongings. Art moved his clothes around inside the sports bag looking for the torch and Traveller's Map but soon discovered they were both missing.

Outside, a crowd of Brillion residents had gathered, including Amy and Mr Beagle.

Art placed the Brillion Village Cup inside his sports bag, closed it and walked outside to find Hayley standing talking to Amy.

'Oh Art, did you lose anything?' Hayley asked.

'Er…someone stole my torch and a map I kept in my sports bag Aunt Hayley,' said Art looking at Amy.

On hearing Art, Mr Beagle immediately growled and walked away sniffing the ground to search for the missing torch and Traveller's Map.

'I did talk to my friend who is a member of the parish council earlier today about Slade's Crew,' Hayley said. 'She has just told me some men from Brillion went to Mill Lane today and apparently inside a building they found Brillion's treasure hunt prizes and some personal items belonging to people who attended the fun weekend. They also found Farmer Calloway's Basset Hound and the missing Shiz-tzu dog locked in a small building.'

Art looked worried as Hayley continued talking, explaining how Slade's Crew were being linked to the disappearance of pets held for ransom right across Oxfordshire and how they had left Brillion in a hurry.

Art and Amy looked at each other, both knowing that without the torch Art couldn't open the gateway to Dragon Valley and Dragons might find a way to come to Brillion to find Spiky.

They both knew everyone would be in danger if that happened.

CHAPTER TWENTY

THE ESCAPE

Meanwhile, just outside Brillion, the Police were scanning the countryside for Slade's Crew. They found their van abandoned not far from Mill Lane and believed they were trying to escape on foot. They set up road blocks on all three roads leading in and out of Brillion so they could stop and search vehicles. They also brought in a Police helicopter to fly over the fields hoping for some sighting of Slade's Crew.

As the Police searched Mill Lane they found evidence that Slade's Crew had been involved in stealing pets for ransom right across Oxfordshire using fake identities and advanced technical lighting equipment to create a distraction. The Police carefully recorded all evidence ensuring nothing was left unaccounted for.

The missing Basset Hound and Shiz-tzu dog had been returned back to their owners and with the help of Mr Popkiss, the Police identified the treasure hunt prizes including some of the personal items belonging to people attending the fun weekend.

The Police told members from the Parish Council they were confident they would capture all four men from Slade's Crew quickly and without fuss, but they did ask for the postponement of the Midsummer Night's Ball until all the men from Slade's Crew had been safely captured.

The Parish Council agreed, but Mr Popkiss feeling guilty for hiring Slade's Crew, vowed not to let this spoil the remainder of the fun weekend. He also volunteered to help reschedule Midsummer Night's Ball to a different day.

News quickly spread throughout Brillion over the incident at Mill Lane and the decision to postpone the Midsummer Night's Ball.

Gradually visitors left the village leaving Art, Amy and Mr Beagle to find a way to help Spiky return back to Dragon Valley.

CHAPTER TWENTY-ONE

WAIT FOR ME

Back at 'Honeypot Cottage', Art was sitting on his bed wondering if the Police would find and return his torch back to him before the time came for him to go with Amy and Mr Beagle to Oak Meadow.

He stared through the open window, deep in thought, looking into the deep green leaves hanging delicately from the branches on the trees. One by one they moved gently as the wind blew causing a rustling noise amongst the trees. This continued for several minutes with Art spellbound by the peacefulness until he was unexpectedly moved by Mr Beagle nudging his side. Art moved his head to look at Mr Beagle. He smiled at him placing his hand gently on his head.

'It's ok Mr Beagle,' said Art, still smiling at him.

Mr Beagle now sitting upright, leant against Art, wagging his tail and barked as he looked directly at the window.

Art feeling very peaceful, diverted his eyes towards the window. A louder noise soon sounded from between the trees as Spiky flew up and down and in between the branches causing leaves to drop down to the ground.

Art got up from the bed to go to his window. On seeing Art, Spiky took the opportunity to show off his flying skills as he flew exquisitely between the branches, heading for Art's bedroom window.

When he arrived he perched himself on the window-sill and released a piece of folded paper from his mouth into Art's hands. Art looked at the paper and he could tell straight away it was the Traveller's Map.

Art smiled at Spiky who was struggling to balance himself on the window-sill.

Mr Beagle still sitting on the bed, barked quietly to greet Spiky.

Spiky made a squeaking noise back at Mr Beagle, causing a puff of smoke to discharge from his nose. He wobbled, looked at Art and released his grip of the window-sill to fly back over towards the trees.

Art sat back on his bed opened the Traveller's Map and in front of him was a message from Samuel.

Art,

Not everyone is who they say they are. Mr Beagle will know how to help Spiky return back to Dragon Valley.

See you later…

Samuel

Art watched as the message from Samuel evaporated. Just at that same moment, Hayley shouted to Art from downstairs, letting him know she was going into the village to help her friends prepare for the final day of the fun weekend.

Art acknowledged his Aunt Hayley, shouting back to let her know that he would be going out as well. He checked his watch realizing it was nearly time for him to go and meet Amy at the bottom of the back garden. He closed his window, put the Traveller's Map in his pocket, then walked downstairs and into the back garden, with Mr Beagle following close behind him. As he walked, he looked up at the trees holding onto the peaceful moment he had earlier.

He continued down the lawn until he reached the bottom of the garden. Waiting for him on the other side of the garden fence was Amy with Spiky, who was sitting on a crooked fence post. Amy looked at Art. She could tell by the look on his face he was worrying about something.

While Art climbed over the fence Mr Beagle jumped through a gap in the fence and ran over close to where Spiky was resting.

'Are you ok Art?' Amy asked.

'Er…yes, I suppose so. I'm just puzzled at the message I received from Samuel earlier,' Art said.

'Another message?' Amy said.

Art held the Travellers Map out in front of him and started to explain to Amy about the message from Samuel, when he saw Marlock some distance ahead disappearing into the forest followed by Star.

Mr Beagle raised his back and growled loudly,

making Spiky wobble on the fence post and causing him to flap his wings to steady himself. Mr Beagle took one final look at Art and Amy, before setting off to Oak Meadow. Spiky followed, flying just above Mr Beagle to protect him.

'Wait for me! Mr Beagle,' shouted Art loudly, waving his arms in the air.

'Come on Art, follow me,' said Amy, starting to walk. 'It won't take long to get to Oak Meadow.'

'Good, I just hope Mr Beagle isn't going to do something silly,' Art said.

CHAPTER TWENTY-TWO

TRAPPED

When Art and Amy got closer to Oak Meadow they slowed down and stopped just inside the forest, looking for some sign of Mr Beagle and Spiky. As they waited, Amy explained to Art where the open area was that she believed Samuel was talking about.

They looked across at the area waiting and hoping Mr Beagle and Spiky would soon appear.

Moments later Marlock walked from the side of the forest followed by Star into the open area. He stood in the middle of the open area with his back to Art and Amy. He held his right arm out in front of him holding something in his hand and started to speak in a language Art and Amy didn't recognize. Star sat on the grass near him observing.

After several minutes Marlock stopped speaking, placed his arm back down by his side and turned his body to face a different side of the forest.

Art and Amy looked on as Marlock held his arm out again and continued to speak.

They could see him much more clearly and what he was holding in his hand.

They watched as Marlock held the torch out in front of him, trying to open the gateway to Dragon Valley.

'It was him. He broke into the sports building, not Slade's Crew,' Art said.

'That doesn't surprise me,' Amy said.

'I'm going to get it back from him,' said Art, starting to walk forwards.

'No…Art, stay here, it's too dangerous,' said a man, standing behind them.

Art and Amy both turned around to look only to find Samuel standing behind them. He looked older and his white beard was longer.

'But…I don't understand,' said Art, pointing at Marlock.

'Marlock is not who he says he is. He's more than a magician. He does have some magical powers, but he is from a different place and time and does not belong here in Brillion. Unfortunately, he's seen an opportunity to enter Dragon Valley, but handled carefully I'm sure we can persuade him to go back to where he belongs,' Samuel said.

The discussion was broken up by Mr Beagle running into the open area barking at Marlock. Spiky soon followed, swooping very close to Marlock.

Star stood up, but chose to ignore Mr Beagle and walked away to sit by the side of the forest near to where Art, Amy and Samuel were hiding.

'Go away, Mr Beagle,' shouted Marlock loudly,

waving his arms in the air.

Mr Beagle continued to bark, trying to distract Marlock while Spiky swooped even closer to him.

'Star, where are you?' Bellowed Marlock angrily.

Star ignored him, sitting down on the grass to watch.

Marlock held the torch out in front of him one last time, pressing the button again and again to try and open the gateway to Dragon Valley.

Mr Beagle continued to create noise and distraction when finally Marlock stopped holding the torch out in front of him, losing his concentration for a moment.

Spiky seized the opportunity and while Marlock was looking in disapproval at Mr Beagle he swooped to snatch the torch with his claws from Marlock's hand.

Marlock swung round to see Spiky holding the torch tightly in his claws, flying away in the direction of where Art, Amy and Samuel were hiding. When he arrived, he dropped the torch on the ground next to Samuel's feet. Samuel bent down and picked it up.

Marlock was furious and turned to face Mr Beagle who was still standing near to him, barking, but not quite so loudly.

'This is your fault Mr Beagle,' said Marlock angrily, raising his right hand in frustration.

On seeing this, Samuel walked out from the forest into the open area. Art and Amy followed, but slowly. Spiky also flew over from the forest to hover near to Samuel, watching Marlock carefully.

'Now, now Marlock, he's only trying to help,' said Samuel, walking towards him.

Marlock put his arm back down by his side and looked at Samuel.

'Help! He's nothing but a menace,' Marlock said.

Mr Beagle ran over to greet Samuel, wagging his tail fast.

'Well done Mr Beagle,' said Samuel, patting his head gently with his hand.

'Give me the torch Samuel,' said Marlock, seriously.

'You know I can't do that Marlock,' said Samuel, holding the torch out in front of him but directly at Marlock.

'What do you think you're doing…no! No!' Marlock shouted.

'It's for your own good,' Samuel said.

Samuel pressed the button on the torch and as Marlock was still shouting, a three-dimensional image of a dark and mysterious place where people were walking around wearing tall pointed hats and long green cloaks, appeared around him.

He was trapped, going back to his own mysterious world.

Samuel pressed the torch again and as the image slowly evaporated Marlock disappeared, vanishing into the image.

CHAPTER TWENTY-THREE

DRAGON VALLEY

Art and Amy joined Samuel in the middle of the open area along with Mr Beagle as Spiky hovered above them. Art thanked Samuel for helping and made a fuss of Mr Beagle for his bravery. Amy joined in, fussing Mr Beagle while Samuel walked over to see Star who was still sitting at the edge of the forest all on his own.

After a short while, Samuel returned with Star who immediately joined Mr Beagle sitting on the grass. They sat next to each other exchanging quiet barking noises to each other.

Samuel looked at Spiky who had now decided to land on the ground near Mr Beagle and Star. Some smoke and small flames came out of Spiky's nose and mouth as he moved around them observing what they were doing. As a precaution, Mr Beagle tried to tuck his tail away from Spiky.

'The time has come to open the gateway to Dragon

Valley. Who would like to open it? Would you Amy?' Samuel asked.

'Oh, no, not really, let Art do it,' said Amy, walking to stand next to Art.

'Are you sure Amy?' Art said.

'Yes, you should do it. I'll watch, probably from over there,' said Amy, pointing to the edge of the forest.

Art laughed and agreed to open the gateway.

'Excellent, here you go Art,' said Samuel, handing him the torch.

Spiky made some squeaking noises at Mr Beagle and Star, before flapping his wings to lift himself back up into the air.

Art pointed the torch and pressed the button on the side. Everyone, including Spiky who was now hovering just above him, waited for the gateway to be opened. At first nothing happened and then without warning, an image of Marlock appeared in front of Art reaching out trying to grab the torch from Art's hand.

Instantly, Art pressed the button on the torch again and in a flash, Marlock disappeared again only to be replaced by a three-dimensional image of Dragon Valley.

'Well done Art, there must have been a malfunction,' Samuel said.

Art focused, holding the torch very still.

Spiky got really excited as he could see Dragons flying around in the image in front of him.

'Get ready Spiky, nearly time for you to join your family again,' Samuel said.

Moments later the image flickered and Spiky knew it was nearly time for him to re-join his family.

'Now Spiky,' Samuel shouted.

Spiky flapped his wings fast, let out some big puffs of smoke and flew into the image to go back to Dragon Valley.

Art watched Spiky fly into Dragon Valley to be joined by two very large green and yellow Dragons. He seemed to remember one of them from the startling image that appeared before him when he tried to use the torch to light up his bedroom recently.

Art continued watching as Spiky flew with the other Dragons deeper into the Valley before pressing the button on the torch to make Dragon Valley disappear.

CHAPTER TWENTY-FOUR

UNTIL THE NEXT TIME

'Good job Art,' said Samuel, looking very pleased.

'Er…Thanks,' said Art, offering the torch back to Samuel.

'No…Art, keep it for the next time,' Samuel said.

'The next time?' said Amy, walking towards them.

'The next adventure,' Samuel said.

Star got up from the ground and stood next to Samuel. Mr Beagle joined him and then went to stand next to Art.

Samuel looked at Mr Beagle and smiled at him.

Samuel put his hand in his pocket to remove a slightly smaller torch.

Art and Amy both looked at him with puzzled looks on their faces.

'A newer model,' said Samuel, holding the torch out in front of him. 'Until the next time.'

Art and Amy watched as he disappeared in front of

them, taking Star along with him.

Shortly afterwards Art, Amy and Mr Beagle walked back to the village and to their cottages.

The next day, the final day of the fun weekend, was as popular as the previous days and everyone went out of their way to enjoy themselves.

The Police made an announcement that Slade's Crew had all been captured which pleased Mr Popkiss and meant the Midsummer Night's Ball could go ahead, but now at an earlier time of 6 pm.

Art was worried about the Ball and made excuses to Amy that he had left his best clothes back at home in Oxford.

Amy ignored Art and made him take her to the ball anyway.

*

On Monday morning Art's mother came to collect him. After thanking Hayley for letting him stay, he gave her the Brillion Village Cup to keep, which made her very happy. Art made a big fuss of Mr Beagle and promised him he would be back to see him again soon. He made arrangements to keep in contact with Amy, then left with his mother to travel back to his home in Oxford.

ABOUT THE AUTHOR

Peter Kavanagh is the author of the Art Myatt
children's adventure series.
Peter lives in Oxfordshire with his wife Maggie.

8426152R00069

Printed in Germany
by Amazon Distribution
GmbH, Leipzig